LOVE,

THE GOD'S

PHILOSOPHY

Vol. 2/3

A philosophical and romantic story. (Based on my life)

Contact us:
booklovethegodsphilosophy@yahoo.com

All the scientific references or not are at the end.

INDEX (SUBTITLE)
(This index represents all volumes)

	SHIVER
	DID SHE DIE REPENTANT?
	A BOOK
	WE ARE INDIGN
	JESUS, MORE THAN POETRY
	THIS IS THE SECOND BOOK
	IT'S TIME TO SLEEP
	WHAT IS THE NAME OF THE BOOK?
	WEDDING
	NOBODY WILL STOP ME FROM WRITING THE BOOK
	LOVE

RELIGION TO SHUT UP AND DEVOUR

Zilda: Religion is very useful for shutting people up and deceiving them.

(They didn´t comment anything about the logic)

Reinaldo: It really is. False prophets have done this, they use religion for their own profit, and they deceive: ***"But beware of false prophets, who come to you clothed like sheep, but inwardly they are devouring wolves"***. (Matthew 7: 15) In Matthew chapter four we can see Satan using the Bible to try to deceive even Jesus Christ.

Zilda: Devourers, in what way?

Nilvana: ***Woe to you, scribes and Pharisees, hypocrites! For you <u>devour</u> the houses of widows,*** *and under pretext make long prayers; therefore you will receive greater damnation*. (Matthew 23:14)

[illegible]: In other words, they took longer than they should, until get the time of any meal and so they devoured the food.

[illegible]: But today you devour something that is not edible.

[illegible]: How do you devour something that is inedible?

[illegible]: By collecting money beyond needs without social commitment.

[illegible]: kkk

SEEMED TO BE DIFFICULT

[illegible]: How do the immaterial connect with the material? (Body and spirit).

[illegible]: What you mean is body and soul. ... ... No, no. You are right spirit is immaterial and soul is life. I don't know how to answer you.

[illegible]: Then ask someone.

[illegible]: The same way software is connected to hardware.

[illegible]: kkk, sorry!

THE EVIL DOESN'T END

Zilda: Why did God send the flood to eliminate evil from the earth? It didn't work! The evil returned soon after. God should have known this would happen, so why did he bother? (Robsin Dhiego Valerio)

Reinaldo: If He hadn't eliminated humans in the flood the world today would be much worse. He allows a limit of evil, the evil grew so much and there was the flood (before the flood Noah preached repentance for 120 years, thus demonstrating God's love, longsuffering and patience), grew again and He divided the world through language at the tower of babel. Then, the laws, the judges, the prophets, finally Jesus Christ and Jesus sent the Holy Spirit. God has always been working for humanity, fighting against the evil, calling for repentance. This increase of evil these days is one of the reasons that make me believe that Jesus is coming back. For love of humanity, He has always given us new chances.

JESUS DID NOT WANT TO REIGN

Carlos: If Jesus Christ was King as you said, why didn't he let the people make him king? Then everyone would believe in Him. (John 6:15)

Nilvana: He said that his kingdom is not now from here, it is not yet time for Jesus to reign here, but he will reign soon, in the millennium. (John 18:36) (Revelation 20:04). Men always want to conquer by imposing force, authority or fear. But Jesus wants to be loved for what he is and not by imposing force, authority or fear. He wants to be loved by people with a true and loving heart and without interest. In the same way a son loves his father for the simple fact of being his father and not for what his father gives him. Unfortunately there are several types of Christians; some are in church just for financial interest or position. But no one can deceive the Lord. He sees our intentions.

RELIGIOUS PRACTICE EVIL AND GOD KILLED

[illegible]: With or without religion we will always have good people doing good things and bad people doing bad things. But to find good people doing bad things, we need religion. (Steven Weinberg)

[illegible]: I've seen something like this on TV...

[illegible]: ...God sent Joshua to kill. It seems to me that old story that says: If we kill some, we are murderers, but if we kill thousands we are heroes (Charles Chaplin). In a survey the following was asked: Would you approve Joshua to invade a country to kill and possess its riches at God's command? The result of the survey was: more than ninety percent of Christians approved the invasion. Another survey was done, but we changed the name of Joshua to the name of the president of the United States. We asked in the following way: You would approve that the United States invades Iraq, kill people and possess their oil. More than ninety percent of Christians did not approve. Conclusion: They approved to kill in the name of God, in the name of religion. The survey revealed that people would not approve of death, but for religious reasons we can kill. They have killed more in the name of God than in the name of anything else. That's why I said that with religion even good people do evil. They even killed a man for taking firewood on Saturday (Numbers 15:32-35). Killing the Jews was a job for God (Adolf Hitler).

Nilvana: This is shocking to say the least. Death shocks man too much. Death does not shock God. For Him death is like sleep. The true dead to Him are those who have died without turning to Him. As for Joshua killing in the name of God, we have some reasons. 1) This way God would be protecting his people from enemies (self-defense). 2) The people that God chose would not learn the customs, traditions and would not follow their gods. 3) **If man kills is sin, but if God kills is not sin. For the simple reason that God gave life and He is the only one who has the right to take it.** 4) Killing people who are getting lost will prevent the descendants to continue getting lost. 5) As for killing a man for taking firewood on Saturday. At that time God was generating a nation so that they would fear his name and would like this nation to be born perfect. With the death of this man, God made many others in the future learn to fear his name. These ordinances of God about killing were in the past.

Reinaldo: Let me complement. Paul when he was a religious consented to death and arrested. But after he recognized that Jesus was the son of God and heard his voice, he never supported anyone's death again. Neither did Jesus and his disciples kill anyone. The most important thing is; after Jesus Christ died, God does not want kill anyone else. GOD SENT HIS SON TO DIE IN THE PLACE OF MANKIND, SO HE DOES NOT KILL ANYONE ELSE. God is no longer angry with mankind. What he wants is for mankind to be reconciled with him through the recognition that Jesus Christ is his only son. Jesus paid our debt to God.

[illegible]: There are crimes that are fundable others are not. Add all the bails of crimes that the entire humanity has committed, from those who have died, to those who are the living, and those who are yet to be born. If it were payable, it would be with a lot of money, wouldn't it? No one would have enough money to pay for so many sins and crimes. Jesus' death paid for all this, because the value of Jesus Christ is incalculable. When he died he said: it is finished (John 19:30). Which means; it is all paid for. That is why Jesus Christ is our visa to heaven and not just a passport. ***"For the wages of sin is death, but the free gift of God is eternal life, through Christ Jesus our Lord.*** (Romans 6: 23). All we have to do is: forgive, repent of our sins and follow the love of God revealed in Jesus Christ.

Reinaldo: I am speechless, your knowledge is excellent my girl...

Nilvana: This debate encouraged me to do more research, thank you my boy...

ATHEISTS LIKE TO ASK

Carlos: Focus on the debate! "Killing people who are getting lost will prevent the descendants from continuing to get lost". In this logic my children deserve to die.

Reinaldo: You didn't understand or didn´t pay attention!

Nilvana: Once again I tell you. That was until the Old Testament; Jesus had not yet died for humanity. Today it is much easier to be saved, and in fact salvation is for those who want to be saved.

Reinaldo: Bravo Nil!

WE HAVE OVERCOME THE PREVIOUS DEBATES

Zilda: How to explain then Isaiah 45:7. I form the light, and create darkness; I make peace, and create evil; I, the Lord, do all these things.

Reinaldo: This evil is a consequence of disobedience. In Genesis 1:31 God says that everything he did was good. Then in Genesis 3, because of disobedience, the woman was punished with pain in childbirth. The man had to work to eat and the serpent had to eat dust every day. There are other examples, but I think that is enough.

: It's incredible; I think you are God's lawyers. You've already started answering questions that were not answered in previous debates.

: God does not need a lawyer, we do, and Jesus is our lawyer. He is the one who justifies my sins by the blood shed on the cross. God does not need to be defended, because He will continue being God without impeached. Defending God's name is good for my growth in faith and knowledge.

RELIGION AGAIN?

: 1) I hate religions, they separate us. Imagine the world without religions, without separation. It would be one less big obstacle to be a single people. That way we would avoid war, hardly a country has war with itself. It would be like the song "IMAGINE" by ex-Beatle, John Lennon. 2) Two Christian leaders, one from each nation blessed in the name of God the soldiers to war against each other, which of the two leaders will God attend? 3) The Christian symbol is a madness, a man nailed on cross. 4) Whoever believes in a triune god, can believe in anything.

: 1) God did not want religion or separation either. In the book of Genesis we can see the division of "religion". Man heard God's voice, and he went down to talk with man. Unfortunately, one day man heard another voice and obeyed. He obeyed a direction contrary to God's will. He followed another way of life, another philosophy of life, another "religion". 2) Again? I have already said that God does not order to kill anyone else because he sent his son to die in the place of humanity. 3*) But we preach Christ crucified, which is scandal for the Jews, and madness for the Greeks. But for those who are called, both Jews and Greeks, we preach Christ, power of God, and wisdom of God. For the folly of God is wiser than men. And the weakness of God is stronger than men* (1 Corinthians 1:23-25). 4) Once Jesus prayed for the disciples to be one, just as he is one with God. Again he said that when we get married we are one flesh. Now, man and woman are two different people, but when they get married they are unique in their dreams, plans, and purposes. In the same way is Jesus and Yahweh/Jehovah, they are distinct, but unique in intention, plans, and purposes.

IT IS NOT MY FAULT

Carlos: Do I understand? So all this mess is happening in the world was for the reason that a man sinned in the Garden of Eden. So Adam sins and I'm the one who pays? Or worse, mankind paid and will pay because of the sin or mistake of one man? What kind of God is this? He makes mankind pay for another man's error? Where is justice?

Reinaldo: If I were Adam and Nilvana were Eve, we would do the same or worse than that. For one man sin, condemnation and evil entered in the world, but also for one man entered the forgiveness of sins, the love of God and salvation. His name is Jesus Christ, the Lamb of God who takes away the sin of the world. This world is not fair because it is being guided by human beings, God is just.

THE FORBIDDEN TREE

Carlos: Why didn't God forbid them to eat the fruit of another tree?

Nilvana: Carlos, pay attention, the tree He forbade was the only one that would cause damage. It is not logical to forbid something innocuous, the prohibition was to avoid the knowledge of evil, the knowledge of good they already possessed.

GOD SUPPORTS DIVISION

Bira: Back to talking about division. You claim that division was because of man's sin. How do you explain then, God dividing the world in several languages? The Bible says that there was confusion, so God is the cause of confusion.

Reinaldo: God wanted the earth to be a unique country. He wanted us to be strong. He wanted everyone to be prosperous. All of us with the same rules and laws so that everyone would respect each other, without having differences in customs. Unfortunately, because of man's turning away from God, the evil did not stop growing. Before the tower of babel there was only one nation, commanded by one man, Ninrode. All their bad intentions could be made much faster, with no other opinion contrary to prevent it. Imagine if humanity had only one leader. This leader would be a god, he would have absolute power. As the British historian John Emerich Edward Dalberg said: Power corrupts and absolute power corrupts absolutely. When God divided the languages, he was dividing and weakening the evil present in humanity. It was like a great "fire", so God spread the "embers", weakened the "fire", and only did not "put out the fire" because they were his beloved creatures. He did this for love; He always tries to help us, try deliver-us from the evil, even without deserving it. The history of Jesus is marked by division; He was the man who divided the history into before and after Christ. Read the gospel of John, you will see Jesus dividing the opinion of the people several times.

Nilvana: You got an A.

Carlos: Jesus said that he came to bring separation. ***"For I came to set the man against his father, and the daughter against her mother, and the daughter-in-law against her mother-in-law***. (Matthew 10:35).

Reinaldo: The idea is the same as in Genesis 11. When people in a family accept Jesus' way of life, the family is divided. They are divided between those who want to do their will and those who do not. Imagine if Christianity was led by one man, and it almost is, isn't it? Suppose this man is wrong with his doctrines, then he could influence all Christians to make mistakes. For this reason division or separation becomes beneficial. When there are several leaders there will also be different doctrines and so there will be the questioning about which leader is with the truth, so they will end up seeking the truth and who seeks the truth will find Jesus Christ. We can make a comparison, the economists say: do not put all the eggs in one same basket. If the basket falls down they will break all the eggs, if you put the eggs in two or more baskets the probability of saving some will be higher. In a fallen world the best option is to separate, because if you unite, the evil will be stronger.

THE TWIN TOWERS

Below is an observation that does not belong to the debate was just one of my reflections.

The twin towers fell on September 11th of two thousand and **one**. Now look at what is written in Genesis, book number **one** of the Bible, 11:09. *That is why it was called Babel, because there the LORD confounded the idioms of all the earth, and from* *there the LORD scattered them over the face of all the earth".* (Genesis 11:9). The fell day was on **September 11** coincides with the chapter and verse **11:9** where he talks about the tower of Babel, and two thousand and one coincides with book number one, Genesis. Maybe the terrorists based on this chapter to mark the date of the twin towers' attack. It would be good for the FBI to base locations and dates of attack on verses to predict dates of possible future attacks.

Nilvana: As for separation, I've never heard anything like it.

HOW MANY COMMANDMENTS?

Zilda: For me nobody obeys the commandments. In fact, there are not only ten. Its 613 commandments, you know. No one can love his neighbor as yourself, loving the enemy, is chimera.

Nilvana: Interesting, sometimes Jesus and atheists say the same thing. Jesus also said, **"No one obeys the commandments. Didn't Moses give you the law? And no one obeys the law** (John 7:19). That is why Jesus came, to fulfill the law that no one can fulfill. As for 613 commandments this includes suggestions, but the commandments are ten and were given to the Israelites. After Jesus the law of love is followed, the one who loves forgives, does not steal, does not kill, does not commit adultery, etc. As for the love of enemies, no one needs to love the enemy as a friend. If you can speak well of him, then speak. If there is an opportunity to speak badly thinks about him, do not speak anything. Do not desire bad things, try to forgive them, if you cannot forgive ask for help from God, as Jesus said in the Lord´s prayer: if you forgive, your Father will also forgive you (Matthew 6:9-13). Forgiveness is not only for you to feel good. But to forgive means to set free, let them go, forget the evil they did to you. While you don't forgive the person gets stuck with you, in your mind you sleep and wake up with them, then release them, let them go.

HELL?

[illegible]: I believe you want to help. But consider this. God wants to send you to hell, but He loves you. It's a bit contradictory, don't you think? I think you are more ethical than your God. Take this example: If a snake killed your mother, would you throw it into hell for eternity? How do you love a god who acts like that?

[illegible]: Not everyone is a child of God.

[illegible]: ???

[illegible]: We are all God´s creations; all of us are children of God by formation. We are all brothers and sisters by Adam. We will only be children of God by imitating Jesus Christ. For example, spiritual beings, evil spirits and even the devil are children of

God because He created them. The children that God considers his own children are those who receive Jesus into their hearts, believe in Him, and love Him. ***But all who received him gave them the power to become children of God, those who believe in his name*** (John 1:12). Even Jesus called some Jews devil's son, because they were doing only their own will. ***You have the devil for father, you want to satisfy the desire of your father*** (John 8:44). Read this comparison. A father was stolen several times by his son; objects were disappearing from his house. When he found out that it was his son, he did not want to believe. How could his beloved son, whom he had cared since his birth is stealing him? Disappointed, when he meets his son after knowing these facts, he said: Son, you? I would never imagine that you would be able to rob me, I don't recognize you, you are no longer that child who only gave me joy, you are no longer my son, I don't recognize you. So it happens with God, He created everything and everyone, but He does not recognize everyone as a child, when we behave this way.

Carlos: How can we be happy in heaven knowing that people we love are suffering in hell? A believer told me that the memories we have of loved ones are erased so we don't suffer in heaven. But if we lose our memory, we don't stop being ourselves'? (Robsin Dhiego Valerio)

Reinaldo: There are people who say that everyone will be saved. Others say there is a purgatory, based on Luke 12:59 ... ... Others believe it is real or just a parable, based on Luke 16:19-31, the parable of the rich man and Lazarus, others say that some will be saved by fire, based on 1 Cor 3:15. Or, hell means grave and not a place of torment for eternity. However, if you have received God's love in your heart there is no need to fear hell; I hope that not fearing hell will make you give freedom to the flesh, to sin. What kind of love you received in your heart? From God? I'm a little confused on this subject.

Milyssa: Those who are condemned will only be resurrected when it is time to be judged and cast into the lake of fire, where the second death is. While the save people are enjoying salvation, the condemned dead will still be dead and will only be resurrected after the millennium (Revelation 20) there will be the second death in the "lake of fire". And death and hell were cast into the lake of fire. ***This is the second death, the lake of fire.*** (Revelation 20:14) ***And fear not those who kill the body, and cannot kill the soul; but rather fear him who can cause both soul and body to perish in hell.*** (Matthew 10:28) The death of the soul will be God's mercy for those who have been lost.

Reinaldo: There are controversies, but I am inclined to believe that your answer is the most convincing. Compared to myself, I don't like to see even an insect suffering, I prefer to kill it. And God is infinitely better than us. For me, Revelation 20 makes this very clear. The heaven is not for all, the hell means graveyard, in conclusion: there will be death for eternity or life with God our beloved Father for the eternity. For love of God reveled in Jesus I can´t believe in hell anymore.

Zilda: If there is no hell, people can turn away from God. They won't be afraid of Him anymore.

Reinaldo: The opposite can happen too. What kind of father likes his children to love him for fear? That's the devil; I wouldn't take pleasure in this son. I have a daughter, Carla, and I would like her to love me simply because I, as a father, love her. Not because I can give her a gift or punish her.

Nilvana: It should be terrible to know that someone will die forever, desperate. Even so, it's better to die than to live eternally in torment.

Reinaldo: Maybe, I don't know for sure, when Jesus said there will be weeping and gnashing of teeth, it could be that moment when the dead will know that they will die forever. There are moments that seem eternal, for example, if I put my finger on the fire for 30 seconds, that moment will seems eternal.

Reinaldo: Nilvana, can I ask you a question that might disturb your spirit?

Nilvana: I got afraid, but that's okay. If I can't, help me.

SHE WON'T GO TO HEAVEN

Reinaldo: What would you say to God if on the day of the final judgment he said to you: Daughter unfortunately you will not be saved; you do not have my approval for eternal life. You will be thrown into the lake of fire right now, where the second death is.

Nilvana: I would say, Lord, to me, it's a shame to hear that from you, I have failed. I knew your love revealed through Jesus Christ and I did not correspond to it. Forgive me; forgive me Father, if you said that I do not deserve salvation it is because I do not deserve it. The heavens will be a better place without me, thank you for everything that happened to me, good and bad. Goodbye forever my father.

WE HAVE TO "BEAT" GOD

Reinaldo: With an answer like this, God would go back to the decision. The only way to beat God is with humility.

Carlos: Beat God?

Reinaldo: Beat God in the sense that He can go back with the decision He made, hardly God goes back, but with humility and for love of someone He can go back, forgiving.

Nilvana: Jesus was defeated by a Canaanite woman when she worshipped him. (Matthew 15: 22:28). God was defeated by King Ezekias, also when he adored him. (II Kings 20: 1-6). God was defeated by the Ninevites when they repented. (Jonah 3: 2-10)

Reinaldo: God likes to be overcome by the humble and by those who repent of their sins.

Zilda: Something similar has already happened to me, sometimes when want to punish my children, they come to me, hug me, cry, apologize and they say: I will not do anymore mom. My mother's heart cannot stand it and I forgive them.

Carlos, realizing that Zilda was moved, said

Carlos: Excuse me, but we have to continue with the questions already programmed, ok?

Everyone answered, okay, let's continue.

THE CHURCH IS GREEDY

Zilda: The church is greedy, near my house there is a church that has more than 10,000 members and wants more.

Reinaldo: If the leader is thinking only about the financial part is a sign of greed, but if he is thinking like Jesus about saving souls, it will always be little. Let's suppose that the planet has eight billion and one of inhabitants. If the church of the Lord Jesus had only eight billion, it would be little, because he wants everyone to hear the gospel and be saved. ***What do you think? If a man has a hundred sheep, and one of them goes astray, won't he go to the mountains, leaving the ninety-nine in search of the one that went astray?*** (Matthew 18: 12).

Nikana: Rei, it's already 9:50 p.m., only 10 minutes before you start working.

Reinaldo: Thanks for warning. Unfortunately I have to work now. Tomorrow we will continue. Is it ok?

Rei: Fine, see you tomorrow! Just for the record I also try to love as much as possible.

Reinaldo: How nice! I had already realized that, until tomorrow then.

Nikana: Rei, did you notice that this debate is easier than the first?

Reinaldo: Yes, I agree with you, but Mr. Rosário, asked questions beyond the green file.

Nikana: Yes, they even rebuked them for it. Come on, we still have to finish this one, the yellow, with Mrs. Zilda. Then there's the red one and the X file.

Reinaldo: As for the X file, I got a bad feeling, it's scientific.

Nilvana: Why? Do you think it will have difficult questions?

Reinaldo: Not only difficult, but a subject I have never read about. I'm even afraid of losing faith.

Nilvana: What can't kill us will make us even stronger. (Friedrich Nietzsche)

Reinaldo: I know it, an example: if you knock down a tree, the fallen leaves will serve as fertilizer for it to grow even stronger.

Nilvana: Great comparison, let's fight the good fight.

Reinaldo: Nil, remember that I am at Vasp; I need to leave the "room". Ok baby?

Nilvana: All right, see you tomorrow! Kiss!

Reinaldo: Kiss! See you tomorrow!

My God how many questions, she made me hotheaded. The next day as usual I called Nilvana.

-Good morning Nilvana!

-Good morning Reinaldo!

-I'm worried about the x-file questions, it's scientific.

-Don't worry about it.

-Would you like to see a spectacle of nature?

-Yes, is it an eclipse?

- No, look out your window, it is raining.

- Is it? kkk, you silly. Sorry, but it is true, it is really a show and it is so necessary for our life. Nilvana commented.

THE INCREDULITY OF THE DISCIPLES

-You know, when I read the gospels I notice that the people of Jesus' time were more incredulous. Jesus made the dead rise, the paralytic walk, the blind see, the mute speak, and cast out evil spirits. All these miracles were not difficult for Him, but the great challenge for the Master was to make the people believe that He was the son of God. *When Jesus came to the parts of Caesarea Philippi, he asked his disciples, "Who do people say the Son of man is? They said, "Some, John the Baptist; others, Elijah; and others, Jeremiah, or one of the prophets. And Simon Peter answered and said, "You are the Christ, the Son of the living God.* Everyone thought that Jesus was just a prophet, and unfortunately many think until today. When he asked his disciples the question, only Peter answered, because the disciples as well as the people had doubts. ***Jesus said to Philip, "Don't you believe that I am in the Father, and that the Father is in me? The words I say to you I do not say of myself, but the Father who is in me does the deeds***

(John 14:10). That is, they lived with Jesus for three and a half years and had doubts; imagine us, who have never lived with Jesus, making an atheist believe. It is difficult, not impossible.

HUMILITY

-Imagine if the whole world followed Jesus, how it would be better. He was very humble; when they called him good, he said that there is only one who is good, God is good.

-Very humble indeed. Imagine, one day you got home and saw the following scene. The Queen of England was washing your clothes, Prince Charles was sweeping it and the President Joe Biden was ironing. -Compared Reinaldo.

-What do you mean?

-It would be an act of great humility, wouldn't it? But Jesus did much more than all of them. The King of kings, the King of the universe became man and still served us. If he came as King of the world, it would be a great humility. He, who has the mastery of everything, is worthy to receive strength, honor, power, majesty, and wealth forever, He for whom all things were made. Through Him, and unto Him, and by Him all things were created. He preferred to come poor to oppose the philosophy of this world. They thought, to be a leader, and many still think, people would have to be born with characteristics such as:

tall, white, with blue eyes, thin nose, etc. Jesus, the greatest leader of all times didn't have such characteristics, none of it. With this he proved that everyone can be a leader. For many people of that time, Jesus was a second-class citizen for not being born in Rome. If it were today, it would be as if Jesus was born in a third world country, a second-class citizen. Many today would like to have the "Green Card" (a type of authorization to travel to the United States whenever they want) to become US citizens, to be first class citizens. We "Christians" already have a better "card" than the "Green Card". God has already prepared a city for us in heaven. We are heavenly citizens. ***But now they want a better one, that is, the heavenly one. That is why God is not ashamed of them either, of calling himself their God, because he has already prepared <u>a city</u> for them*** (Hebrews 11:16).

-How humble our Lord Jesus is!

-He even compared himself to a chicken, you know? - asked Reinaldo.

-What? Are you just kidding, aren´t you. I've read that he compared himself to an eagle and a lion, but not a chicken.

-I'm not kidding, look at this verse. ***Jerusalem, Jerusalem, who kills the prophets and stones those who are sent to you! How many times have I*** *wanted to gather your children, as a hen gathers her chicks under her wings, and you didn't!* (Matthew 23: 37).

-Ah! I have read this, of course. What love! Ah, if we Christians had the full conviction of this great love for us, we would live better and much happier.

-Sorry Nil, but I need to go to sleep. Remember that I work at dawn.

-So you don't want to talk to me anymore? Nilvana asked.

-No, not at all. I'm really tired.

NILVANA DON´T STOP TALKING

-I was just kidding, I know you're tired. What do you say we see a movie?

-I was thinking about it. Have you ever seen the ...? - asked Reinaldo.

-No. There was no one to go, but now I can go with you.

DOES THE BAD BEAT GOOD?

-I can say the same thing. Go alone is boring. Nilvana, have you noticed that in every movie good always wins evil? And did you know that this is not always true?

-You always surprise me! But isn't it always right that good beats evil? Considering that God is good and the devil is evil. Consequently we will always have the victory of good for the reason that God is greater. -Nilvana commented.

-Considering God and the devil of course. God is the only Being who is above good and evil. God is not the good, He is above the good. God never fought with the devil. We can see in Revelation 12:07: ***There was then a war in heaven. Michael and his angels fought against the dragon, and the dragon and his angels fought back.*** It was the Archangel Michael who fought with the devil, not God. In Revelation 20:1-2 it says that one angel, only one, and not an army of angels, will arrest the devil for a thousand years. ***And I saw an angel coming down from heaven, having the key to the abyss and a great chain in his hand. He arrested the dragon, the ancient serpent, which is the Devil and Satan, and bound him for a thousand years***. Lucifer was Cherubim, second in the heavenly hierarchy, lost to the Archangel Michael, seventh in the heavenly hierarchy. It was a great humiliation; the worst of it is that Satan will still be arrested by an angel, who is the last position in the heavenly hierarchy. I understand that it would be cowardice, God, the almighty, to fight with his creature, but there are evil spiritual beings stronger than good spiritual beings (Daniel 10:13). In Revelation 11:3-12, says that Satan will overcome the two witnesses of God, so everyone will think that Satan is good because he won the witnesses of God. His victories and his defeats are not proof that God is or is not in his favor. Because God is not in favor of only one country, religion or much less in favor of a soccer team. Never ask God for a proof of love, God already proved that He is in favor of humanity when He gave His only son to save us.

RAPTURE OR ABDUCTION BY ETS

-It's good to talk to you. I always learn something interesting. Speaking of movies, a friend of mine who watched the rapture movie told me that when Jesus returns and rapture the church, that is, when millions of people and all the children in the world disappear. Governments may say it was the aliens who abducted the people.

(If you are not raptured there will be reason to despair, but there will be hope, a second chance to be saved, do not submit to the mark of the beast).

-I am also zzzzzz (I was falling asleep) learning a lot from you.

At this moment I started to sleep on the phone. I had already told Nilvana at the beginning of the call that I was tired, but she kept talking.

-zzzzzzzzzzzz.

-Rei, are you there?

-What? Yes, we can watch this one about ETs. Which actors attend this movie?

-kkk. Reinaldo you didn't pay attention. I said that when the day of the rapture comes, they will say it was an alien abduction. -Commented Nilvana.

-You're right; they will say things like that. The big difference between a supposed ET abduction and the rapture will be that all children, without exception of race, religion, color, ethnicity, will disappear, because they are innocent and pure.

DOES ET EXIST?

-Do you believe in Et?

-For me the Ets are those heavenly beings who fell with Satan, the unclean spirits. All creatures that exist outside of our planet are extraterrestrial. The heavenly beings and the unclean spirits also fit. Jesus said, ***"You are from below, I am from above; you are from this world, I am not from this world"*** (John 8:23). I have heard people with a good mind, with credibility and a high degree of education saying that they have seen UFOs in the company of several people. - Reinaldo commented.

WE ARE SPEAKING THE SAME THING WHITH DIFFERENT WORDS

-Talking about Ets, I was reading one of these days there are atheists scientists who admit the possibility of life could started with the participation of Ets. I understand that in their radicalism in denying the existence of God they end up appealing to the Ets. Maybe we are talking about the same thing, but changing the word God for the word ETs. -Nilvana said.

-I didn't know that, it's a way to admit God in creation without admitting it. Because as you studied, you noticed that life cannot have started by itself, it is crazy to think that something so complex simply evolved without the participation of God.

-About the rapture you clarified my doubt. I wouldn't know how to differentiate between a supposed alien abduction and the rapture.

-Zhatzt zizht. (that's right)

-You have a funny voice; it sounds like you have a cold.

-No, I'm just a little tired.

-Why? Oh, I'm sorry; I forgot you're tired, you work at dawn. Good rest and see you tomorrow. - Apologized Nilvana.

-Till tomorrow then, bye.

-Bye and see you tomorrow!

Now I fainted from tiredness on my bed.

SATAN ROUND TABLE

Someone dreamed the following dream: There was a meeting, Satan and his angels are planning a way to get Jesus out from people's hearts, and the conclusion was this: Replace Jesus with religion, customs, rites, etc. Overload them; make them hate the Christian religion. ***For they bind heavy burdens that are hard to bear, and put them on men's shoulders; but they do not even want to help them with their fingers*** (Matthew 23:4). After that men will hate religion, and since religion is confused with Jesus, it will be easy to take Jesus out from men's hearts.

ANOTHER EXPERIENCE WITH GOD

Around 5pm I got up. When I got out on the street, I saw some people handing out tracts about Jesus' words. I remembered an experience with God. In 1995 I dreamt that I was handing out some tracts to my neighbors. When I looked down the street, I saw a sign in the sky. There was a number on the sign. I don't know if it was 500 or 5,000. When I had this dream I didn't understand anything. The curious thing happened in 1999. I felt a strong desire to hand out tracts with Jesus' words to my neighbors. So I wrote a letter with three themes: Can we believe in the Bible? Why should I go to church? (If it is a church where the New Testament is preached much more than the old and the love of God is above all, it is worth attending that church). Who is Jesus? It was late December 1999. We were entering the year 2000, and Brazil would be 500 years of discovery, I took advantage of this date and put in the title of the tract: "Brazil is 500 and you still do not know how to answer these three questions?" After I delivered the tracks I remembered the dream I dreamt in 1995. In the dream I was delivering the tracts with the words of Jesus and I saw the number 500, that is, I would evangelize my neighbors in the year 2000, when Brazil would be 500 years old.

Chapter 5 - the yellow file (PART 2)

WHAT IS THE DIFFERENCE?

Again I arrived at Vasp an hour early for the debate.

I entered the "room" and Mrs. Zilda was already there.

Reinaldo/Nilvana: Good evening, Zilda. Good evening Carlos

Carlos: Buenas noches!

Zilda: Good evening, I am about to finish my participation in the debate. I'd like to ask two questions right away. 1) According to the Bible was the devil who gave the option of good and evil and why do you say it was God? 2) What is the big difference between a good atheist and a good Christian?

______: 1) God said that they should not eat from the fruit of the knowledge, the good and evil fruit. But the serpent said that they could eat. So because of this you believe that God did not give the option of good and evil, but the serpent. In fact, man already knew good and they ate the fruit only acquired the knowledge of evil. It causes only loss. He did not stop man from sinning, but advised him not to sin by not eating the fruit. It was a mistake, because they already knew well. 2) A good Christian should never feel good. As a Christian I should always try to do well, even for those who don't like us. A good atheist can be as good as or even better than a Christian. God has the vision of "X-ray", He knows who is and who is not.

ADAM AND EVE DID NOT DIE AS THE BIBLE SAYS?

______: In the Garden of Eden, God said that the couple would die if they ate the forbidden fruit; the couple ate and did not die. Did God lie?

______: It was a spiritual/intellectual death.

______: Could you be clearer? You always have an answer for everything, don't you?

______: Yes, I'll give you an example: A man earned a salary of 50 thousand dollars per month, lived very well, and had three wonderful houses, one for housing, and another in the countryside and another on the coast for the weekends. He had employees to take care of his houses; he had five cars and so on. One day he got involved with drugs, became addicted, as time passed he lost his job, friends and family because of his addictions. He started to accumulate debts, sold the houses and cars to pay off his debts. Finally he became a beggar, ate leftover food, he hadn´t money even take a bus. So he "died," that good socioeconomic and comfortable life that built his psyche, no longer existed.

Reinaldo: That's happened to the Adam and Eve, that communion with God they had, that feeling of loving and being loved by God, the life they lived in the paradise of Eden, with abundance, security without need to work, no longer existed. Imagine the psychological effect they suffered, they became totally different people, and they died spiritually and psychologically.

Nilvana: That's more or less what happened to you Zilda. When you lost that awaited job, you ended up losing a big part of your dreams, that joy and pleasure of living, that level of social life that you enjoyed and no longer enjoy are good comparisons with Adam and Eve who "died". I am sorry for your loss.

: You made me understand better now. Do you believe this happened because I stopped going to church and God punished me?

BAD THINGS HAPPEN TO GOOD PEOPLE

: No, I don't believe it was God's punishment, we are in a bad world and bad things happen to all of us, with good and bad people, with religious people or not.

: I don't consider myself bad!

: No, I'm sorry, that's not what I meant, we are all bad in God's eyes and we know how to do good things. Even so, God wants to save us.

: What is the difference between a bad Christian and a good atheist?

: When a bad Christian recognizes that he is bad, he will please God. Because he is aware that he needs to improve and he needs God's forgiveness. But when a good Christian recognizes that he is good he will not please God.

: Why not?

: Because nobody is really good by God's standards. A young man called Jesus good master and He said: **Good is God** (Matthew 19:17). Another example is the parable of the Pharisee and the publican. The Pharisee (religious), proud, prayed advantages about himself, saying that he prayed and fasted, and the publican said he was a sinner and was not worthy to look at the sky. Jesus concluded by saying that was the publican, the sinner who was humble, who pleased God and not the Pharisee, religious and proud (Luke 18:10-14).

Reinaldo: I remembered a proud brother, saying that he went to travel by car with his friends, there was an accident and the four friends died and only he survived. He proudly said that God had delivered him from death and not the others; he was feeling himself special, above the others who died. I don't believe that as a rule. It could have been God or not, I believe that it is very rare that God would deliver only some of very serious accidents. Whoever survives should not be proud; he should not think he is more important than the others.

Nilvana: Based on this, I could observe that there are many people outside the church who are pleasing God more than some inside the church. Many in the church are talking about themselves like the Pharisee. At the same time that someone talks about themselves, they are exalting themselves; he will humiliate the one who listens. What is the difference if I said: I am great. Or saying: you are small. What is the difference? If I said: I am a man of God. Or saying: You are not a man of God. I fasted so many days... I prayed so many hours... I went to the mountain to pray. I, I, it's a lot of "I" and me. Why say: I will travel to that country. Since there are people in the church who have no money even to visit a relative in another state. ***He who speaks of himself seeks his own glory; but he who seeks the glory of him who sent him, that is true, and there is no injustice in him***. (John 7: 18) I believe that even the offerings decrease when people hear this. They preach against envy, but they are producing envy in the people´s heart. The human being is already born with envy, the problem is when envy consumes you and you start wishing evil on your neighbor or when you want to take possession of something from your neighbor.

[illegible]: So there is not much difference between atheists and Christians. We are almost the same.

[illegible]: It's true, we are <u>almost the same</u>. We can see this in the parable of the weeds and the wheat. And I am not saying that the wheat is the Christian and the weeds are the atheists, because only God knows the deepest part of our hearts. These two plants are very similar. Maybe men cannot see the difference, but God has "x-ray" vision, He knows who is and who is not.

[illegible]: Let me finish the debate. I have been thinking a lot about this, sometimes I see some Christians acting like atheists.

WE ARE PIGS

Reinaldo: Imagine that we are all pigs. Every pig likes mud, likes to get dirty. So we all are atheists and Christians like mud. Jesus said that all those who hear His words are being cleansed (John 15:3). That is why those who reads the Word of God and receives it in his heart is "washing himself", we need to "bathe", because we are "pigs". We must always do what is right more and more and make mistakes less and less. The church that preaches the Words of Jesus, a serious church, is also a place to "cleanse" ourselves. There we hear words like these: love, forgive, repent of sins and believe that He is the son of God who died for our sins. These words "fix" us, "cleanse" us. Conclusion: Those who pray, and read the Bible every day are like "pigs" who bathe every day. Those who do not seek God are like "pigs" who never bathe. We are all "pigs", but one takes a bath and the other does not, so we are similar. That is why we must seek God.

Carlos: What a humiliation, comparing us to pigs in the mud.

Reinaldo: When a human being is in the "mud" of sin he is even more "dirty" than a pig in the mud. It is not humiliation, it is a comparison.

IS THIS LOVE?

Zilda: You mentioned one of the main doctrines of Christianity is love. How do you explain to me

Christian leaders who are enriching and preaching love to others, see people starving and do nothing? What kind of love is it?

Nirvana: All the churches I have attended until today have always witnessed that there is a social department to help the neediest people. Many donated to charities, recovery for drug addicts, etc. They don't always say what good they do because it is written: **when you give alms don't let your left hand know what your right hand has done. So that your alms will be given in secret and the Father who sees in secret will reward you publicly**. (Matthew 6:3-4)As for religious leaders getting rich with the money collected in the church, I have no words to describe it, is monstrous upwards.

THE JUSTICE ABOUT IT

Zilda: Good things happen to bad people and bad things to good people. Even with Christians tragedies happen. He allows evil to happen even with Christians, this is only one of the reasons why I don't believe in God.

Reinaldo: It's true, it happens. The first righteous man was killed by his own brother. Cain killed Abel. The Bible speaks of a man who turned away from evil, was a servant and feared God, but a great tragedy happened to him. His name was Job. (Although after the turbulence had passed he became richer than before) Another man performed miracles, signs and wonders, when he spoke he showed amazing wisdom. He left men confused with his intelligence. They beat this man, almost died with the beating. They crucified him on a cross, agonized with pain until death. His name is Jesus Christ. Everything that happened to these men was simply for the reason that they were righteous living in a land of the unrighteous.

Nilvana: We can see this in politics, with a rooted corruption, a caste. If someone honest enters, they may even die. I think it's very unlikely that anyone honest will enter politics.

Reinaldo: Unless they are willing to die.

GOD LEFT HIS SON ON THE CROSS

Zilda: Let me continue with the questions. Why didn't an almighty God take his son off the cross?

Reinaldo: ... **and without bloodshed there is no remission.** Hebrews 9:22. ... **who was rejected by the elders and chief priests and the scribes, who was killed, and after three days rose again**. Mark 8:31. Jesus already knew that he would be killed, that was his last goal. He came to die in the place of mankind, so that we have the right to eternal life. God could have taken his son away from the cross. He is the almighty, he could give an order. But He didn't do anything; sometimes doing nothing is the most difficult. This is proof that God can control his great and absolute power. Many rich and "powerful" men cannot control the power they have, but on the contrary, the power controls them and this does not happen with God.

INTEREST

[illegible]: If Christians had a "perfect" life I would also be a Christian.

[illegible]: How easy it would be to be a Christian and have a perfect life. Everyone would be converted, but not because of the God´s love. It would be for the pleasure of having a "perfect" life. Only when we suffer for what we love, we give proof that we really love it.

PRAY

[illegible]: I don't know how I stand you! You are answering my questions with simplicity. Answer me, is God omniscient?

[illegible]: Yes, He is.

[illegible]: If God is omniscient, he knows everything. So why do we have to pay?

[illegible]: When we are praying we are speaking to Him. Who has no pleasure in talking with whom they love? Who doesn't like to spend time with the one we love? That is why we should like to pray. God rejects prayer from the exalted (Luke 18:11-14), if you want to be heard by God, be humble, not wishing the evil to anyone or even your enemies. Be careful when asking for something for your benefit, there are things that benefit you and harm others.

GLORY OF HUMANITY

Zilda: 1) Our history, the history of humanity is too big to believe in a supposed God. 2) I love the glory of humanity, look at all the technology we've developed so far, we've been to the moon, it won't take long and we'll be on Mars. The tendency is always to go further.

Reinaldo: 1) Do you want to stand beside history because of greatness? Stay on the side of God who is greater than everything and everyone, He is greater than the universe. And the history of humanity is not bigger than our planet. 2) Many have stopped seeking God because they love the glory of humanity. *For Demas forsook me, loving the present century, and went to Thessalonica, Crescent to Galatia, and Titus to Dalmatia.* (II Timothy 4:10) When we will be with God in eternity we will be like angels (Luke 20:36) and all this technology will become useless.

DIFFICULTY IN BELIEVING

Zilda: Maybe I don't prove to you that God doesn't exist. Neither do you prove to me that God exists.

Nilvana: Zilda, with all these questions answered, do you still not believe? There are people who believe because of a simple opening of a flower. There are people who don't believe even if they see God face to face. Two people can see different things looking at the same object.

Zilda: I remembered something I saw the other day. Two people were looking at a picture that showed beach chairs on an empty background. It was asked for first. What is missing from this picture? He answered: Obviously the sea is missing; I only see the beach chairs and not the beach. It was asked the same thing for the second person. She answered: Of course people are missing, I only see empty chairs.

Ronaldo: Don't you realize that we are a miracle? When you see yourself in the mirror, can't you believe in the miracle in front of you?

Zilda: If you tell me that your grandfather was cured of cancer I would tell you: So what! I won't believe it even for this reason. Some friends told me that I will convert to God when I am about to die. But I have already prepared myself for this moment. I asked some atheist friends to be my witnesses to prove that I did not convert. If I am on a hospital bed to die, they will be there. I asked them to film me so I will say: I died atheist, God does not exist. That's enough for me; it was very good to debate with you. Thank you.

50

Reinaldo: Wait, I know that at least you believe in the historical Jesus, the Jesus-man, who was born at the time of the Roman Empire. God sent his son in order to the unbelievers could see to believe.

Zilda: You Who Have God in Your Life can see God in everything, but I don't have God in me, so I don't see God in anything. I liked the debate. Thank you!

Zilda: You left the "room".

Carlos: Until the next debate.

Carlos: He left the room.

THE END OF THE YELLOW FILE

Reinaldo: Maybe she is still in the "room" just watching. Pray to God Zilda; ask Him to reveal Himself to you. Speak the truth, say you can't believe. Even the Jews did not believe in Him. The almighty Lord God who delivered the people from the power of Egypt could not be that carpenter from Nazareth they said. A people who know the Bible very well could not identify "their" God. ***But I tell you that many will come from the east and the west, and will sit at table with Abraham, Isaac, and Jacob, in the kingdom of heaven; and the children of the kingdom will be thrown into outer darkness; there will be weeping and gnashing of teeth*** (Matthew 8:11-12). There are people who have never seen each other in person; they only know each other by telephone or the Internet. When they meet they recognize each other. The "people of God" could not identify them. I know that sometimes it is difficult even for the Christian to believe. Do you know why? In Revelation 12:12 it is written: ***"Woe to the inhabitants of the earth! For the devil has come down to you, and he knows he has short time.*** We have a great enemy to overcome and the only way to overcome him is with the word of God (Matthew 4:4) and unfortunately you do not believe.

: Easy Rei, rest a little. Save your energy for the last debate. There are still two files, the red file and the X file, which is scientific.

: Nil, I am so disappointed none of them believed in God, what a deep sadness.

: Remember you said at the end of the other debate, the seed was planted if it falls into good soil, it will grow and bear fruit.

: Thank you for reminding me of this, it is my consolation. I am a little afraid with these two files that are coming.

: Don't worry about it. The difficulty can be relative, maybe what they find difficult, can be easy for you.

FUTURE

Reinaldo: Or vice-versa, right? But what are you doing now?

Nilvana: I'm watching a film about time machine.

Reinaldo: How about if we could go back to the future?

Nilvana: What? Are you talking about that old movie from the 80s?

Reinaldo: No. The future we almost all hope for is to retire, have a good life without having to work, with peace, security, maybe living in a beach house, or on a farm. Imagine the quiet. Listen to the birds singing, eating fresh fish, lying in a hammock, breathing fresh air, climbing mountains and so on. God had already prepared all this for man, there in the Garden of Eden. But now we are living with fear, insecurity and peaceless. What would the world be like if we didn't need to invest money in things like these? What God had already prepared is the future we all want. That is why we need to go back to the future, because the future is behind us and not in front.

TIME TRAVEL

Nilvana: I don't think I've ever heard that. The future is behind us and not in front.

Reinaldo: At some moments in life I felt myself back in the future.

Nirvana: How was that?

Reinaldo: One time or another, when I close my bedroom door and read the gospel of Jesus, letting those words enter my mind and heart, when I cry feeling His presence, feeling His great love for us. In these moments it seems that life is perfect and that we have no problems.

Nirvana: It is true, when I am too happy or in love, it happens. If we really felt God's love for us, just as He really loves us, we would feel strong at all times. We would overcome anything in life. Speaking of the future, is there any biblical verse that God can travel through time?

Reinaldo: I have heard a theologian say that God is present in all three times, past, present and future, for Him there is no time at all, for Him it is as if everything that has happened until today is just one day.

Nirvana: Do you know any verse in the Bible talking about this?

Reinaldo: Yes, for example: Behold, I will turn back ten degrees to the shadow cast by the declining sun on Ahaz's clock. So the sun went back ten degrees to the declining sun (Isaiah 38:8). See also this other: And the sun stood still, and the moon stood still, until the people took vengeance on their enemies. Is this not written in the book of Jasher? So the sun stood still in the middle of the sky, and did not rush to sunset, almost a whole day (Joshua 10:13).

NO CINEMA

Carlos: Excuse me! I'm sorry to disturb your romance. But I was wondering if you'd like to continue the debate?

Reinaldo: Yes, let's continue.

Carlos: The next one will be Mr. Sydney, a Brazilian who lives in Sydney, Australia. He will enter the "room" for the debate tomorrow.

Reinaldo: All right, I believe that time I will need Mr. Silvano's help.

Carlos: It's confirmed. You are already in the middle of the debate; I believe that you are not one of those alienated Christians.

Reinaldo: Thank you! Jesus was not one either. He questioned the religious of his time a lot. God asked Job several questions from chapter 38 of the book of Job. ***Where were you when I was founding the earth? Let me know if you have intelligence*** (Job 38:4). Jesus wanted to make the religious thinker, but instead they gave more importance to traditions and rituals than to God's main commandments. It is love, faith and mercy (Matthew 23).

Carlos: I learned that we have something in common, the love for people. See you tomorrow then, at the same time and in the same "room".

Reinaldo: Until tomorrow.

Nilvana: No! Reinaldo, you said we would go to the movies tomorrow. Could you cancel the debate?

Reinaldo: Forgive me! Carlos, are you still in this "room"?

Carlos: Yes, I understand. But he has a business trip scheduled for next week and if he doesn't start soon he won't have time to finish until the day of the trip. Could you cancel the movie? Why don't you go a little earlier?

Nilvana: I can't. I arrive from work around seven o'clock at my house. Until I get ready and leave, we'll arrive at the cinema around nine o'clock at night.

Carlos: Is the cinema that far from your house?

Reinaldo: It's not just 5 minutes. Don't you know that women take a long time to get ready? Nil, I'm sorry, but we're going to cancel the cinema, only this time, I want to end this debate right away.

Nilvana: All right then Rei, let's schedule another day.

Carlos: Thank you! See you tomorrow then.

Reinaldo: See you tomorrow.

Nilvana: See you tomorrow Carlos. Rei, I remembered that tomorrow has a birthday party. Could you come by my house to go together?

Reinaldo: All right, can it be at seven? I just can't stay until the end because I have to work and leave home early for the debate.

Nilvana: Yes, it can be. Bye and see you tomorrow then. Kiss.

Reinaldo: Kiss. Bye.

The next day as usual I called Nilvana.

WHERE IS NILVANA

-Good morning! I'm worried about the x-file issues, it's scientific.

Mrs. Nilza, Nilvana's mother, was the one who pick up the phone.

-Don't worry about it. That's how Nilvana answers you, right? Kkk.

-Mrs. Nilza!!! Good morning.

-Good morning son. She already left to work.

-She left early?

-Yes, she told me she needed to go earlier to participate in a meeting. She forgot to tell you and apologized.

-All right, I'll be there around eight o'clock to go to a birthday party.

-She told me that she will go to this birthday party and will arrive later, by 9pm. don't be late or I will be worry.

-I can't be late, I have to work. I have to arrive early to start another debate. Then I'll leave her at home around 9pm.

-I hope so son, you know how mothers are, right?

-Yes, mothers are all the same, they just change their names, addresses and appearances. Thanks Mrs. Nilza, see you later.

-See you later and good rest, God bless you.

-God bless you too. Bye.

-Bye.

Chapter 6 - The Red File (PART 1)

LET THE SEED GROW

The next day, will be another debate day. I prayed, asking Jesus to give us intelligence and grant us wisdom to answers every question, in order to some of them can believe in Jesus and turn to God. I know that the word of God is like a seed. Some seeds are born quickly, others may take a long time to be born, depending on the kind of land it was scattered. Have you seen what happens when the concrete of a sidewalk cracks? Plants or bushes begin to appear. Why? Because the seed was there, just waiting for the sun to rise. In the same way you, we must all sow the seed of Jesus' gospel. Show Jesus' love, sooner or later the seed you planted will be born. You plant it, someone else rules it, and God will give it to grow (1 Corinthians 3:6). I arrived at Vasp and went into the chat room.

Reinaldo: Good evening Carlos.

Carlos: Good evening Reinaldo. Mr. Sidney is already in the "room". Good luck for all of us.

Sidney is from São Paulo, lives in Sydney, Australia. He already was religious, as his parents as well. He has an IQ of 140; he likes to mock religious people with his questions that ridicule the Bible and God. His great pain and sadness was not to have married with the love of his life and that's why he decided to move to Australia. He has hoped to end up with a family, but is worried because is reaching middle age.

Sidney: Good evening Reinaldo. Can I start with the questions?

Reinaldo: Good evening. Yes, you can.

Sidney: First open your e-mail. I sent a photo.

SHUT YOUR MOUTHS

Fortunato: Reinaldo, what is this photo he sent you?

Reinaldo: It's a picture of a dinosaur and it's written like this: Shut up Reinaldo! I don't know what he meant.

Fortunato: I know what he meant. Sidney, that's not what we agreed, we had talked about it before. Mr. Rosario from the green file also acted like that, he asked questions that didn't belong to him. Reinaldo disregard this photo for the proper time.

Reinaldo: Why?

Fortunato: Because it's subject of the X-File. We will talk about evolution.

Sidney: I'm sorry, but I didn't resist. kkk.

Fortunato: Fine, but let's proceed as we had agreed.

IS IT GOD'S WILL?

Sidney: There's a verse in the bible that makes me understand that all that happens is God's will. I base it on the following verse: ***Don't you sell two little birds for a farthing? And none of them will fall to the ground without your Father's will*** (Matthew 10:29).

Reinaldo: A lot of people do not understand this verse very well, neither do I. There are two kinds of God's will. The first is absolute will, what He determines no one can change. The second is the permissive will, for example, He allowed the Adam and Eve to eat the fruit that He had forbidden. In the Father's pray Jesus said that God's will is done only in heaven and not on earth. ***Your kingdom come, your will be done on earth as it is in heaven***. (Matthew 6:10). In heaven, spiritual beings live according to God's will, but here the will of men with the influence of evil is done. It is not God's will that there should be factories of cigarettes, of weapons, so that people would die early. It is a mistake to think that everything is God's will. Once a friend hit his colleague in the face and was fired. When he was fired he said: God knows what he does. People act wrongly, suffer the consequences of their actions and think it is God's will.

TERRIBLE THINGS

Sydney: 1) So He is allowing many terrible things.

2) Why disability children are born. Has God made a mistake? Why does God allow children to be born to die afterwards?

3) Why doesn't God answer prayers?

4) Why so much hunger in the world?

5) Why doesn't God heal amputees?

6) If God exists, I deserve to die. I am evil.

7) If God existed we would not grow old or die.

8) Where was God when the twin towers fell?

Reinaldo: There are many questions; I will number the answers according to your questions. 1) The problem is that man has "turned his back" to God and does not accept His advice. Mankind elected Satan as the god of this world. ***"I will no longer speak much to you, because the prince of this world approaches, and has nothing in me;"*** (John 14: 30). And also this other one who says***: "The god of this world (Satan) has blinded the minds of the unbelievers, so that the light of the gospel of the glory of Christ, who is the image of God, may not shine to them"*** (2 Corinthians 4:4). He allows what man decides, whether good or evil.

2) ***"And the Lord said unto him, who made man's mouth? Or who made the dumb, or the deaf, or who sees, or the blind? Is it not I, the Lord?"*** (Exodus 4: 11). God made the disabled too. Now I will tell you, if you do not believe in God because of some children who are born disabled, then you will have to believe in God for the billions of children who are born perfect. When children are born and die in a few minutes later, we are in a fallen world where children, youth and adults die every day.

3) In this verse below shows what we must do for God to answer the prayers***. Is it not also that you***

share your bread with the hungry, and gather the abandoned poor at home; and when you see the naked, cover them, and do not hide your flesh? Then shall thy light break forth as the morning, and thy healing shall spring forth speedily, and thy righteousness shall go before thee, and the glory of the Lord shall be thy rearward. Then you shall cry out, and the LORD will answer you; you shall cry out, and he will say, 'Here I am. If you take away the yoke from the midst of you, stretch it out from your finger, and speak wickedly. (Isaiah 58:7-9)

You ask, and you do not receive, because you ask badly, to spend it on your delights. (James 4:3) *But seek first the kingdom of God and his righteousness, and all these things will be added to you* (Matthew 6:33).

4) This one I answer with the first.

5) I believe that he heal amputated, I have seen miracles with my own eyes, not at this level. But I have heard reports of people who had one leg smaller than the other and one leg equaled the other.

6) He is patient; he will give many chances for people to come back to Him. He is late in getting angry.

7) Nowadays, scientists already say that death can be avoided in the near future. They say that death is a chemical process like the process of life. If men are

capable of this, imagine God. If man had not sinned, we would be eternal. There were three men in the Bible who did not die. Enoch, Elijah and Moses walked with God, and they did not die like the rest, because God pick them up into heaven. If the earth were the kingdom of God, here would be the paradise and we would not die. But His kingdom is not of this world (John 18:36).

8) In the same place as always. In heaven, in his Kingdom, where he rules sovereignly and everyone does his will what is perfect and pleasant. He does not rule this world, but only in the life of those who allow Him to rule. Jesus himself said, ***"My kingdom is not of this world; if my kingdom were of this world, my servants would fight so that I would not be handed over to the Jews; but now my kingdom is not from here.*** (John 18:36) If you do not believe in God by this logic, that the twin towers have fallen, two buildings. Then you will have to believe in God because of the millions of buildings that are standing all over the world.

SHED BLOOD

Carlos: There was no prerequisite for redemption. Why doesn't He forgive without blood? Several animals were sacrificed and then the blood of a man. (Jesus)

Nilvana: There was a prerequisite. It was determined by God, that the offering for guilt or sin was this way. *The animal of the guilt offering will be killed at the place where the burnt offerings are sacrificed, and its blood will be spilled on the sides of the altar.* (Leviticus 7:2.) By offering an offering of the best animal without blemish, God wanted men to understand that He deserves the first place in their lives.

Reinaldo: As for the blood of Jesus, it was because God was already fed up with this kind of sacrifice. And He himself provided an offering for us. *What good is the multitude of your sacrifices to me, says the Lord? I have had enough of the burnt offerings of rams and the fat of fattened animals; I do not like the blood of calves or lambs or goats.* (Isaiah 1:11) ... *Therefore I will give him a portion among the great,[g] and he will divide the spoils with the strong,[h] because he poured out his life unto death, and was numbered with the transgressors, for he bore the sin of many, and made intercession for the transgressors.* (Isaiah 53:12). Jesus fulfilled the law in our place, now we need to walk with a heart willing to forgive, help, repent of sins, let the love revealed on the cross make a deep impact on us and so we will live more according to the will of God.

SINNERS LIVE FOR THE RIGHTEOUS

Carlos: Why didn't God make the one who sinned do not exist?

Nilvana: So there would be no one, because everyone has sinned. ***For all have sinned and fall short of the glory of God*** (Romans 3:23). But those who sin and do not repent will cease to exist. ***And he who was not found written in the book of life was cast into the lake of fire*** (the lake of fire is only a symbol for the second death, the death of the spirit.) (Rev. 20:15)

Carlos: As you said before, God is the only one who can take life because was He who gave it, so if everyone sinned, why doesn't He exterminate the humanity of the earth once and for all.

Nilvana: I just answered. They will be exterminated if there is no repentance. And for love of the righteous He lets the unjust live.

Reinaldo: Abraham questioned God about this when God said he would destroy Sodom and Gomorrah. Abraham said, *"Lord, if there are fifty righteous people in the city, will You destroy the city? God answers, "No, Abraham, for the sake of fifty, I will not destroy the city. Abraham continued asking ... and if there are forty-five ... forty ... thirty ... twenty ... ten.* As in Sodom and Gomorrah there were not ten righteous, but only four, the family of Lot, God ordered their removal and after that the destruction came

Sidney: A friend gave me a sheet with some questions. Some of them are part of my own questions; I will send them to you now.

Reinaldo: You can send them, but remember that I am at Vasp. In case you don't have time to answer them, I'll leave them for tomorrow.

Sidney: I'm sure you'll leave them for tomorrow, there are many.

When he sent me the questions, I was scared. There were a lot of questions, some difficult, others childish.

Reinaldo: I promise I will answer them all. But I can only deliver them on Monday. Today is Friday, tomorrow I go to work. On Sunday I will have time to answer them. On Monday I will give you the answers.

Sidney: All right, until Monday.

Reinaldo: See you Monday.

The next day I called Nilvana as usual.

-Good morning Nil. I'm worried about the x-file issues, it's scientific.

-Good Morning Rei, don't worry about it.

-He sent me so many questions!

-Do you want send me some, I'll help you.

DOUBTS ARE SOMETIMES OURS TOO

-I will send you half; maybe some of them will repent and turn to God when they have their questions answered. Perhaps the effect of the Word will not be immediate, but the seed of the gospel will be there inside them. Have you ever noticed that many questions they asked we, Christians, ask as well? Did you know that this debate is being good for my development in biblical knowledge? Did you also know that behind a problem there is an opportunity?

-Rei, it's true, it's being good to clarify my own doubts. Sincerely my faith has become more solid. And until the end of this debate I believe it will get even better.

-I need to do something to contribute to the Kingdom of God. I don't want to get to heaven empty-handed. I don't want to get there and realize that I missed opportunities to speak the word of God so that someone would be saved.

-You are absolutely right.

-Nil, do you know what I'm thinking now? -No!

A BOOK

-When you told me that it was good for you. I kept thinking, what do you think about helping me write a book about this debate?

-A book? It would be interesting, because if I am a Christian, I felt strengthened by the research and answers we found, whoever reads a book based on this debate will be as well.- Nilvana commented.

-I believe that whoever reads it will become stronger. It will work as a vaccine against lack of faith.

-It will really be like a vaccine. The vaccine is the dead or weakened virus. When the person is vaccinated, the body starts to develop antibodies. When the virus of the disease itself arrives, the body has had time to develop antibodies. So it will be protected against attacks that can even kill a life.

-That's right Nil; the book will be like a vaccine. It is the same as preventing or solving a problem before it happens. Would you help me write a book?

-Yes, let's research more questions and add these questions to enrich it.

INVITATION FOR AN AFTERNOON COFFEE

-We will talk about this later. Now I need to rest, I need to go to sleep. My mother is here beside me inviting you to have afternoon coffee with us, could you come?

-I agree, and if it's possible I'd like to help you answer those questions from Mr. Sydney personally. Nilvana commented.

-Good, bring your bible.

-All right, can it be around 2:00pm?

-Perfect, it's confirmed, a kiss and bye.

-Goodbye, I wish you sleep well, with the God's protection. Kiss.

COFFEE WITH PHILOSOPHY

I printed the questions on a sheet. Some questions disturbed me. I called Mr. Silvano, the theologian, to help me with some questions. His cell phone was in the mailbox, I couldn't talk to him. I managed to answer some questions and the others I left to answer together with Nilvana on Sunday. Nilvana and I started to answer the questions. Until my brothers José and Angelo arrived and asked what we were doing. I answered that it was a debate. They advised me not to get into debates with atheists, it is dangerous, and you could lose your faith they said. I answered that I had already gone too far, now it's not long to finish. And my brother Sydney opened a dialogue with me.

JOSÉ'S QUESTIONS, MY BROTHER

-Some friends of mine have already asked me something about faith that I did not get an answer.

-What were the questions?

-First, let me comment on something. A friend told me that no one can stop attending his first church and attend another one because it is written: ***not abandoning our congregation, as is the custom of many ...*** (Hebrews 10:25)

-What the verse says is this: not to leave the congregation, it does not mean the place, but the act of gathering, to gather with those who have the same faith. This does not mean exactly the act of going to a church, but to be in the midst of people who will help you keep the faith.

NOAH´S ARK

-What do you know about Noah's ark?

-Around the year 1660, some Jesuit priests did calculations to try to find out if Noah's ark would fit the animals, the 1600 species known at the time. It was concluded that it was possible, if we were to consider all the species and animals known today, about one and a half million different species between animals and plants would certainly not fit.

-Oh! Interesting, but how to feed lions, tigers, elephants, giraffes, hippos for so long?

-The region where Noah lived was desert, so it wasn't all the animals we know today that entered the ark, there weren't that many animals, it wasn't a forest where there are several species like: lion, bear, elephant, giraffe and so on. The Bible says that the whole earth, that is, the whole planet, was flooded with waters, but at that time man did not know the whole planet, I understand that the world that man knew at that time was flooded. Until the middle ages, in the 14th century, our continent was unknown, the whole world did not include the American continent, imagine then 4,000 years ago. The Bible is right with the vision of that time. —Reinaldo answered.

Nilvana surprises me with another vision.

-Rei, there is another vision, they say, in the ark only the basic species entered, example: a couple of feline, one of equine, one of canine and so on. There was the "evolution" of the base species or variation. I believe in the micro evolution, that is, variation, when specie continues the same with variation. -Nilvana answered.

-Great, that is great. I didn´t know about it.

PREJUDICE IN THE BIBLE

-Let me continue, a friend of mine told me that the Bible is prejudiced. For example: people with a flat nose, bald or with some deformity could not be priests (Leviticus 21:18-23).-commented Sidney.

-On the other hand Elisha was one of the greatest prophets, he worked signs and wonders and was **bald** (2 Kings 2:22-23). I believe that the priest must be good-looking because of the popular demand. The people like to see the beauty, and they value it very much. That happened with King Saul, God chose for the people a good-looking man, it was not according to God's heart, it was according to the people's heart. He was even the highest among the men of Israel (1 Samuel 18-24). The people rejected God preferring a human king. But God chose David, a man according to his heart (according to his heart for a time without Jesus), with short stature, without the appearance of a king. Because God does not see as man sees, the appearance, He looks at the intentions of mind and heart (1 Samuel 16:7).

MEANING OF LIFE

-It really is, isn't it? What would you answer me about the purpose of man's creation? Or what is the meaning of life?

-There is a biblical theory saying that God made men to replace fallen spiritual beings. There was a vague space to be filled in the heavens, so the Lord made men to dwell in the place of the fallen spiritual beings. For me the purpose of life is happiness, the very perception of life. Have you ever stopped to think that only when people are sad they asked this question? When we are happy we do not remember this question. When the human being is happy he does not ask: Why am I alive? Or what is the meaning of life?

-Maybe I'm wrong, but I think there are more unhappy people than happy people in the world. So the purpose was not fulfilled?

-Many things have not yet been fulfilled, but it will still be fulfilled. God has given us many reasons to be happy, for the simple fact of realizing that we are alive, for being able to contemplate nature, the miracle of life and so on. However living in a world systematized by men, who has time to contemplate nature, the beauty of life, the stars? Due to pollution we cannot even see them anymore. We only have time to contemplate the TV, the cell phone and the internet. We are victims of a world that has turned its back on God.

ANGELO QUESTIONS, MY BROTHER

At this moment my other brother, Angelo, came into the conversation and asked me questions too.

-The question is: why do people who have no commitment to God prosper? And many people who do not seek God prosper? The Christian gets a little unbelieving when he sees the wicked prospering.

PROSPERITY OF UNBELIEVERS

-For me it is a very religious question, influence of the theology of prosperity. If you seek God and do not work you will die hungry. But there are also people who prosper in the wrong way, cheating, stealing and so on. Read Psalm 73, you will see that the psalmist almost lost faith. He saw that the wicked were fat and prospering. The psalmist doubted the righteousness of God, but he understood that the wicked do not have the same end as the righteous. The question is, how are they prospering and how are they spending their money? Jesus' gospel cannot be about prosperity. We must not seek God for what He can give us, but for what He is. Many prosper by natural blessing, self-effort, work harder, and prosper more. A good number of churches today think that way: *You will all know that you are my disciples if you **prosper** more than others who do not attend churches.* When the right thing is*, **everyone will know that you are my disciples if you love each other**. (John 13:35)

-But Reinaldo, God wants to put us by "head" and not by "tail" (Deuteronomy 28:13).

-Read carefully from the beginning of the chapter, God is making a promise to the nation of Israel, if they would keep the commandments. It is not something individual; imagine if all the Israelites were "heads", if all were leaders nobody would work. But you as a Christian know that Jesus came to serve,

He said that whoever wants to be the greatest is the least, the one who serves. He himself said that he came to serve and not to be served. ***For the Son of man (Jesus), did not come to be served, but to serve***. (Matthew 20:28).

WE WOULD BE ETERNAL

-If Adam and Eve had not sinned would be there death?

-I don´t believe, the only tree that God forbade was the tree of good and evil. There was also in the garden of Eden the tree of life, which God did not forbid them to eat, (forbidden after they sinned) if they ate from this tree they would live forever (Genesis 3:22-23).

CATHOLIC CHURCH

-What is your opinion about the Catholic Church regarding the worship of saints?

-Who are we to throw the first stone at the Catholic Church? Who deserves our worship is only God and Jesus. As for the saints we have to respect, most of the saints are our brothers and sisters who already died. Once a man knelt down before the apostle Peter, Jesus' disciple, and he said, "Stand up, I am a man like you. (Acts 10: 25 and 26) Again the Apostle Paul was preaching with his companion Barnabas, and people thought they were gods. Paul and

Barnabas tore their clothes, got naked, to prove that they were ordinary men. (Acts 14:14 and 15) Once a woman knelt before Jesus, anointed his feet, wiped his hair, and Jesus allowed to be worshiped because he is God (John 12:3). But many of us are worshiping the wife, husband, money, car, house, position, college, work, etc. I repeat, who are we to throw the first stone in the Catholic Church? God may help us all.

JESUS REJECTED AND AGAINST THE OLD TESTAMENT

-Why did the Jews not accept Jesus?

-Angelo, there are some reasons. One of them is that they were waiting for a "Messiah-Liberator," who was brave like Joshua, rich and powerful like Solomon. The carpenter from Nazareth, son of Joseph and Mary, did not meet the requirements. Although Jesus had proved by his works, signs, and wonders, to be the Messiah, they did not believe. Jesus said to them, "I have said it already, and you do not believe it. The works that I do in my Father's name bear witness to me (John 10:25).

-In Psalm 1:1 he says: do not to sit with the scoffers, but Jesus walked with all kinds of sinners. It seems that he ignored this verse.

-Jesus had the power to influence people, He was the doctor for the sick (Matthew 9:12). If you can influence your friends with the gospel, stay close to them. But if they can influence you to make a mistake, avoid them.

REWARD

-What do you understand by reward? What kind of reward would it be?

I imagine a gold crown, or precious stones.

-None of that. When the religious were praised, Jesus said, ***"In fact they have received their reward"***(Matthew 6:2).

-What? Is it only praise?

-Yes, but imagine if the Queen of England praised you. Imagine the people, the national and international media looking for you for interviews, you end up playing famous, fame can bring benefits. Better than that, the reward will be when God himself speaks well of you to all heavenly beings.

I finished the conversation with my brothers. We started answering the questions around 2:30 p.m. and we finished around 6:00 p.m. Thank God we were able to answer all of them.

Chapter 7 - the red file (PART 2)

NO DEBATE

On Monday I entered the "room" to continue the debate.

Reinaldo/Nilvana: Good evening, Sydney.

Sydney: Good evening, Reinaldo. I look forward to reading your answers.

Reinaldo: The good news is that I was able to answer them all. And the bad news is that I won't be debating with you today. I typed your questions with my answers below. I am sending you by e-mail. I need to work at this moment, in case you have any doubt about the answers, you can comment them tomorrow. So good night and see you tomorrow.

Sydney: Good night. I'll definitely come in again tomorrow. See you tomorrow.

And this was the question and answer sheet I sent to Mr. Sidney. He was very smart; some questions seemed to be directed at me. But he was inducing me to put my ethics above God's ethics.

From: Reinaldo/Nilvana

To: Mr. Sidney/Carlos

QUESTIONS BY E-MAIL

Below are your questions and my answers with their names.

REJECTION OF THE MESSAGE

Sydney: What would you do with people who don't believe in you or reject you?

Reinaldo/Nilvana: I would find out why they reject me. If I found out that I had done something wrong, I would try to apologize. But if they didn't accept and kept rejecting me, I would just ignore them. I believe that in relation to God is much more serious. Reject God is like rejecting the light and preferring the darkness. And if they prefer darkness, they will "stumble" and not know where they are stepping. If you reject God, you will be without His protection and become an easy target for the darkness.

Sydney: If you had to send an important message, would you send it full of riddles and let them change the message? You must have played telephone already, right? And you know very well that the phrase you say to the first person is not the same one that reaches the last person. Would He leave his message in the hands of people who could distort it and put at risk the salvation of the soul?

Reinaldo/Nilvana: I wouldn't send a message with riddles or let anyone alter it. As for the bible, the "riddles" you mention are the parables or prophecies. We don't need to understand the whole Bible to be accepted by God or to be saved. As for the changes, there was a special care to make the copies. A group of men called Soferim (scribes in Hebrew) wrote down at the end of each book the number of paragraphs, words and letters. If any copy did not have the same number of paragraphs, words and letters they were discarded. Later another group of men, the Massorettes, worried about the quality of the copies and corrected possible mistakes of the Soferim. For this reason four gospels were written to confirm what the other says and to complete each other. Two were disciples (Matthew and John) and the other two were not (Luke and Mark). Even Luke had to do an accurate investigation (like a CBT) because he was going to send a copy to an authority of the time. ***Since many have undertaken to do a coordinated narration of the events that have taken place among us, as those who have been eyewitnesses and ministers of the word from the beginning have transmitted to us, it seemed good to me too, after having invested everything carefully from the beginning, to write you a narration in order that you may fully know the truth of the things in which you have been instructed.*** (Luke 1:1-4) But even so, there are errors in the Bible, especially in the translation from the original, but as I said; we don't need to be experts in the Bible to be accepted by God. God has not left his word to all those who are transmitting, but men themselves for various interests are using it, few are preaching what God really wants.

HOW DO YOU KNOW IF YOU ARE NOT MISTAKEN?

Sidney: If Satan is the Father of Lies, how can we be sure that he has not deceived Christians and made them worship him as god and reject the true god? (Robson Dhiego Valerio)

Reinaldo/Nilvana: Jesus taught that the summary of the law is love, so if I do not love, forgive, repent of my mistakes preferring hatred, rejoicing in vengeance, if I rejoice in evil when it strikes others, I will be doing the will of Satan, and I would be a "Christian" deceived. He who loves is from God.

CHANGE OF RULES

Sidney: If God is immutable, why did he need to "change the rules" by sending Jesus on earth? (Robson Dhiego Valerio)

Reinaldo/Nilvana: Immutable in his power and love, not in his law. For our shake, he changes his own law, a new law, a new covenant. ***This cup is the new covenant (new covenant, the law of love) in my blood, which is shed for you*** (Luke 22:20).

I have noticed several times that since the debate with Mr. Rosario until now, there are questions that are not exactly atheistic, but questions from people who could not believe that God is love.

WHY THEY DON'T UNDERSTAND THE MESSAGE

Sydney: How would you act with people who don't understand your message?

Reinaldo/Nilvana: I would try to send more messages in order they could understand them. Jesus said why some did not understand his messages. ***Why is my language not clear to you? For you are not able to understand what I say***. (John 8:43). At that time Jesus answered***, "I thank you, Father, Lord of heaven and earth, that you have hidden these things from the wise and understanding, and revealed them to the little ones*** (Matthew 11:25).

OMNIPRESENT?

Sidney: If God is omnipresent, why should I look for him somewhere?

Nilvana: God is omnipresent in the sense of knowing everything, that is, in spirit; if not Jesus would not say in the Father pray the following phrase: *Our Father who is in <u>heaven</u>*.

Reinaldo: Well, how can we understand what Jesus said: I am going to the Father? I have come from the Father... ... I will come back... where there are two or more speaking of my name there I will be (in spirit) ... I will prepare a place ... our father who is in heaven. There is a place where God dwells, in heaven. Blessed will be the time when Jesus will return to rule here during the millennium. He will return, that is, He is not here. When Jesus returns to rule the earth all religions will collapse, they will all be extinct, because

God the Son, Jesus, will be here, we will see God face to face.

WHO WRITE?

Sidney: Who wrote the Bible? Was it God or man? Gods are fragile and can be destroyed by science. (Chapmam Cohen)

Reinaldo/Nilvana: If I told a three-year-old child that the mayor of São Paulo did a soccer internship, she would imagine that he did it with his own hands. But in fact there were several people with the appeal released by the mayor. But it's not wrong to say that the mayor did that soccer internship. Following this reasoning is not wrong to say that it was God who wrote the Bible. In fact, it was men who wrote the Bible, but partly with God's revelation and partly simply wrote the events, the news, and the history. I will give only one example among several, proving that it was inspired by God. In Genesis 2:7 it says that God made man out of the dust of the earth. And science has discovered that more than ninety percent of the chemical elements found in our bodies are also in the earth. We are really made of dust. The curious thing is that the book of Genesis is over three thousand years old, it was written when there was no science. As I also mentioned in the previous debate, there are more than 100 prophecies of the Old Testament fulfilled in the New Testament about the Messiah. As for the other question, God cannot be destroyed by science, God is Spirit, and He does not die.

VIRGINAL BIRTH?

Sidney: All the gods had a magical birth, including Jesus, born of a virgin. Kkk.

Reinaldo/Nilvana: 40 years ago the world's first test-tube baby was born, today artificial insemination is becoming more and more common, so how can we doubt that God put his son in Mary's womb.

SIX DAYS

Sydney: How can I believe in the Bible if it says that the world is six thousand years old and all creation was made in only six days?

Reinaldo/Nilvana: The Bible does not say that the earth is six thousand years old. That was the conclusion of some biblical scholars through genealogy. But in Genesis 1:1 it says: In the beginning God created the heavens and the earth. That is, in the beginning it does not mean the first day. When God began creation there were already the heavens and the earth. (There will be a more complete explanation in the course of the book).

REPULSIVE

Sidney: The Bible repulses me for several reasons. It doesn't allow working on Saturday, and many need and work on Saturday.

Reinaldo/Nilvana: Not working on Saturday is for a particular people. ***So the children of Israel will keep the Sabbath, celebrating it in their generations by perpetual covenant*** (Exodus 31:16). The law was given to the Jews until John the Baptist, and not to us, not Jews. ***For all the prophets and the law prophesied until John*** (Matthew 11:13). Christ redeemed us from the curse of the law, making himself a curse for us; for it is written: Cursed is everyone who hangs on a tree (Galatians 3:13). So the law has served us as a servant, to lead us to Christ, so that by faith we might be justified (Galatians 3:24). And again I protest to every man, who lets yourself be circumcised, who is obliged to keep the whole law (Galatians 5:3). Separated from Christ are you who are justified by the law; from grace you have fallen (Galatians 5:4). For the whole law is fulfilled in one word, in this: You shall love your neighbor as yourself (Galatians 5:14). But if you are led by the Spirit, you are not under the law (Galatians 5:18). Which of you will be the man who, having a sheep, and on a Sabbath day it falls into a pit, will not make all the effort to get it out? So how much better is a person than a sheep! Therefore, it is lawful to do well on the Sabbath. (Matthew 12:11-12)

Carlos: What did you do to not have the free will to work or not on Saturday?

Reinaldo/Nilvana: These commandments were to the people of Israel, if they accepted, would become the people of God. But today, with the death of Jesus for our sins, anyone can be God's "people" when we obey the law of love. (He) came for those who was his, and his people did not receive him (The Jews did not receive him). (The Jews did not receive him.) But to all who received him, to those who believe in his name, he gave them the power to become children of God. (John 13:35)

JEALOUSY NO, ZEALOUS AND LOVING

Sidney: God says he is jealous, he does not allow other gods to be worshipped.

Reinaldo/Nilvana: Nobody would like their wife or husband to live with someone else, would they? The Lord also has this jealousy, by the way, Lord means owner. As to the other gods, I said in the previous debate, they are spiritual beings, when they rebelled against God, became evil spirits and were cast out from heaven with Lucifer who became Satan. ***And the great dragon was cast out, the ancient serpent called the Devil, and Satan, who deceives the whole world; he was cast out into the earth, and his angels were cast out with him.*** (Revelation 12:9)

Sidney: If God is jealous, in my opinion, he is not a perfect being, since jealousy is not a good feeling, and we are only jealous if we judge our "adversary" as good, or better than us, it is difficult, since God is all powerful.

Reinaldo/Nilvana: What can I see here is love, in some translations the word jealousy has changed to zealous, careful or loving.

SATANÁS SURGIU

Sydney: God is omniscient, okay, but he didn't know that Satan would appear?

Nilvana: If you knew you would have a son who would give you 50 years of pleasure and only one month of grief, would you have this son? That's what happened, Satan (opponent) when he was Lucifer (full of light) gave many joys in heaven, was like a conductor, organized the songs of praise to God. But now his days were numbered. This question of yours makes me understand that Satan is the great culprit of our miseries. I believe that without Satan man would eat the forbidden fruit in the same way, perhaps some of the descendants of Adam and Eve. We don't need Satan to be evil, on some occasions he ends up accelerating the evil in us; even so the decision is always ours.

Reinaldo: God has set a day to end all evil. There will come a day when evil will no longer exist. I was thinking, who guarantees that there will not be another Satan in the future? In Revelation, God said that he will make new heavens and new earth. When that happens there will be no more evil. I believe that there will not be another Satan, that is, another being that turns against God because they have seen what the result of turning against God was. I understand that God's creation is not yet perfect, but it will be when all the evil is extinguished. Other "satans" will not arise because they know the disastrous result and the condemnation of the first satan. This great evil that God allowed us to give free will, was like a "vaccine" in the conscience of all heavenly beings. In the future, when the idea of being evil comes to mind, it will not evolve because we are aware of the consequences it has caused. So we will surrender our free will and our whole being to God. We will say, perhaps sing a song more or less like this: Let His will be done in heaven (already done), let His will be done on earth (still done), let His will be done in our being, with You Lord, in control of everything we will be complete, we trust in you 100% completely. All we have are Yours, all we are is through you, holy, holy, holy is your name.

LOVE ALWAYS

Nilvana: May his will be done, for the great and infinite love of God when he gave his only son to save humanity.

Reinaldo: Look! I forgot the most important thing, love, thank you honey.

Nilvana: Muchas gracias, guapo. (Thank you very much honey)

Sydney: At the time Satan manifested himself; didn't spiritual beings know that God was love?

GOD WINS BECAUSE HE IS LOVE

Reinaldo: They did know, but you still didn't have concrete proof. When God gave his only son was the definitive proof. ***But God gives proof of his love for us, when we were still sinners, Christ died for us*** (Romans 5:8). It was the great defeat of Satan.

Nilvana: Rei, You know there was a pre-defeat?

Reinaldo: Pre-defeat? I never heard of it.

Nilvana: When God asked Abraham to give his only son Isaac to be sacrificed. It was a representation of God handing over his son to humanity; imagine all the heavenly beings watching this event. Their conclusion was probably the following: *If a man gave his only son for love of God (even though he was freed from death) then, imagine God having a greater love, will he not give his only son to die for humanity?* At this time Satan and his "angels" panic, they understood that God is love, and no one can overcome love.

Reinaldo: You're really something, huh? Have you noticed that always end up with love?

Nilvana: Yes, that's how it should be.

FORGIVE LUCIFER

Sidney: May I continue? Focus on the debate! Why hasn't God forgiven Lucifer?

Reinaldo/Nilvana: Lucifer as Cherub, a spiritual being had a total knowledge of God, knew exactly what he was doing, was not tempted by anyone, the decision to rebel came from himself. He is not like the man who makes mistakes for not having a full knowledge. If man does not repent and insist on error, he becomes "Satan" too. You cannot be forgiven when you insist for doing evil.

HOMOSSEXUALS

Sydney: A) The Bible says that homosexuals have to die. B) I have a friend who doesn't like soccer, but likes fashion. It is commented that He is gay, in my opinion this is not enough to determine a person's sexual choice.

Reinaldo/Nilvana: A) As for killing homosexuals, I have answered before that God doesn't order to kill anybody else; He has already sent His son, Jesus, to die in the place of humanity. B) I also believe that this friend of yours is not a homosexual just because he likes fashion. ***God, therefore, created human beings***

in his image, in the image of God created them: male and female created them. (Genesis 1:27) All of nature was changed when man disobeyed God, all of us are fallen human beings, we are in part victims and also guilty for changing our nature. What does Nil think?

Nilvana: Why do we label people? Sydney's friend was called gay just because he likes fashion. There is even male fashion and female fashion.

(Many people today think that Christians are effeminate because they seek to have sexual intercourse only after marriage and within marriage. They think that to be a saint is to have the appearance of those "holy" images that have the effeminate appearance. But that is not being holy, being holy is looking like God. To be a saint is to be honest, to forgive, to repent of mistakes, to try to get it right more and to make mistakes less. Not to speak evil of others when we have opportunity, but to speak good of others. God is holy let us also be as He is. In my opinion each one chooses the life he wants to live and lives the consequences. For any couple, whether heterosexual or homosexual, I advise them to be faithful to each other, to love each other and not to be promiscuous. Now answering according to the bible is an abomination, contrary to nature and a mistake. (Leviticus 18:22; Roman 1:26-27) Finally, Jesus said nothing about homosexuality. He calls all of us sinners to repentance, that is, we all need to return to His light of love and sincerity.

DEATH TO TEENAGERS

Sydney: Teenagers are punished to death in Deuteronomy (21:18-21. 10).

Reinaldo/Nilvana: Yes, it is written, but it is an extreme case, gluttonous, drunken son who does not listen to his parents even after punishing him. But the power of decision was in the hands of the parents to denounce him. I believe that the parents will hardly denounce him. That was in the time of the law, now we are in the law of Jesus' love.

AMPUTATION OF THE BODY

Sidney: Jesus order to cut members out of the body that makes you sin (Matthew 5:30).

Reinaldo/Nilvana: Jesus was calling our attention to the gravity of sin. Sin is a very serious problem. The only effective solution to sin that God found was through the death of His own son. If there was another solution to the sin, God would not have sent His only son. It's not useful for me to cut out sinful hand if I sin with my feet. Jesus does not want you to cut out any of your members, but he wants us to leave sin. He is willing to forgive us and help us in this war against ourselves. None of Jesus' followers cut out any part of his body and did not even ask anyone to cut it out.

Reinaldo: Nil, how nice of you to help me; let's take a break for a cup of coffee.

Nilvana: Ok, there's tea with lemon too, which one do you want.

Reinaldo: Iced tea?

Nilvana: Yes!

Reinaldo: Very good, very tasty. I'll get some rye cookies too.

After about 15 minutes of break, we went back to answer Mr. Sidney's questions.

IS THE BIBLE MALENESS?

Nilvana: As for this question, maleness in the bible, I have doubts too.

Sidney: The bible is maleness.

Reinaldo: And he said, ***"Therefore, will a man leave his father and mother, and join his wife, and they will be two in one flesh? (***Matthew 19:5) Well, if the two are one flesh, there is no maleness. As for man's dominion over his wife, this was God's punishment for his wife sin, and man's punishment was to work for food. And to the woman he said, ***"I will greatly multiply your sorrow and your conception; in sorrow*** *you will bear children; and your desire will be for your husband, and he will rule over you.* (Genesis 3:16) We can also see Jesus talking to a woman (John 4:7-27), and worse, the woman was a Samaritan, a people despised by the Jews. After the resurrection, Jesus appears first to a woman, Mary Magdalene, and then to his disciples. (John 20: 15-20).

Nilvana: The apostle Paul wrote something maleness. He wrote that women should remain silent in the church.

Reinaldo: 1) It was not a commandment but a suggestion, so, those who spoke the word of God would not be interrupted. 2) Paul was Jewish and even converted to Christ had a Jewish "cargo culting". 3) Men did not talk in the congregation and women did, so Paul wrote that women should be in silence because men were already in silence.

Nilvana: I liked your explanations; I got runaround on that.

ESCRAVIDÃO

Sydney: The Bible supports slavery.

Reinaldo/Nilvana: Slavery was a reality at the time. This does not mean they were mistreated, but on the contrary, God commanded them to have the same rights. *But the seventh day is the Sabbath of the Lord your God; you shall not do any work, neither* *you, nor your son, nor your daughter, <u>nor your servant, nor your maid,</u> nor your beast, nor your stranger, who is within your gates* (Exodus 20:10). A people who had been slaves should treat their slaves well. ***In this there is neither Jew nor Greek; there is neither male nor female; for you are all one in Christ Jesus.*** (Galatians 3:28)

INTERPRETATION

Sydney: The biblical interpretation depends on one's ignorance. (Roberto G. Ingersoll).

Nilvana: They are repeating some questions; they are not organizing themselves very well. But we will answer them:

Reinaldo/Nilvana: Jesus asked them: ***What is written in the law? How do you read*** (or how do you interpret in some translations)? ***He answered him: You shall love the Lord your God with all your heart, with all your soul, with all your strength and with all your mind, and your neighbor as yourself. Jesus said to him, "You have answered well; do this and you will live.*** (Luke 10:26-28) Jesus said that the Pharisee answered well. The interpretation comes down to love for God and neighbor, every time you read the Old Testament, compare it with Jesus' gospels, accept it when fits, if it does not fit it is not for nowadays.

Sidney: Jesus told the Jews to eat their flesh and drink their blood. Did he want the Jews to be cannibals?

Reinaldo/Nilvana: This eating and drinking is symbolic, He was telling us to allow his words to become part of our being. Food and drink are fuels that give us energy and life. Jesus wants his words to be fuel for us too. ***Not only will man live by bread, but by every word that comes out of God's mouth.*** (Matthew 4:4)

CONTRADITIONS

Sidney: There are several contradictions in the Bible: 1) Mark 14:72 says that the cock crowed twice, but in Luke 22:34-60 the cock crowed only once. 2) In Matthew 27:34 Jesus tasted the vinegar but in John 19:30 they said that he drank the vinegar. 3) the book of John 21:6 say that Jesus asked to cast the net after resurrected, but in Luke 5:4 Jesus asks to cast the net before resurrected.

Reinaldo/Nilvana: As the questions 1 and 2, imagine that you have two children and asked each of them to write a book about your life. Will the books be exactly the same? Of course not, one child will remember things that the other did not. So there are little differences, but these mistakes don't disturb us to the way of salvation. As for question 3, what is the problem if they have thrown the nets more than once? I believe that the disciples not only cast their nets twice, but because they were fishermen they were always casting their nets.

We are still answering those questions that Mr. Sidney sent us, he replied some answers. We ended up including them because we wrote this book long after.

ERRORS IN THE BIBLE

Carlos: It's a mistake, and who guarantees that there won't be any more mistakes? Who guarantees that the person who wrote didn't interpret it wrong? Who guarantees that the translation of the Bible really meant that?

Reinaldo/Nilvana: That is why, <u>FOUR</u> gospels were written, so that one could confirm what the other says and complete each other. Two were disciples (Matthew and John) and the others two were not (Luke and Mark). There was no concern to write the book of John in chronological order. Even Luke had to do a thorough investigation, like a CBT, because he would send a copy to an authority of the time. ***So, having undertaken many to put in order the account of the events that took place between us, according to the same people who witnessed them from the beginning, and were ministers of the word, (he took the account of the disciples themselves) it seemed to me also convenient to describe them to you, O***

excellent Theophilus, in your order, having already thoroughly informed me of everything from the beginning; that you may know the certainty of things of which you are already informed. (Luke 1:1-4) (As a complement I mentioned earlier about the Soferins and Massorettes who worked meticulously on the copies of the books of the Old Testament).

BREAKING THE LAW

Sydney/Carlos: God broke his own law. A) When the descendants of Adam were punished. B) When he killed the first-born of Egypt. C) When he punished Jesus for the sin of humanity.

GOD KILLS

Reinaldo/Nilvana: A) The descendants of Adam were not punished; they suffered the consequences of sin. If through one man, Adam, the sin entered into the world, through another man, Jesus, forgiveness of sins entered into the world as well. B) As I have answered in other debates, the one who gave life is the one who has the right to take it. God gave the alert before taking the life of the firstborn; he gave all the chances for Pharaoh to free his people. He took the breath of life away when they were sleeping; he handed it the best way.

Nilvana: There was no violence in the death of the firstborn sons, they were sleeping, it was already midnight. The one who gave his life is the only one who has the right to take it, and he did it in the best way possible, while they were sleeping.

Nilvana/Reinaldo: The worst thing in life is not death, but living without purpose, without hope of meeting God. C) Those who broke the law in truth were men, who offered sacrifices for the remission of sins, but continued to sin. **What good is the multitude of your sacrifices to me? Says the Lord, I had enough of the burnt offerings of rams, and the fat of fatlings; and I do not like the blood of bullocks, or of lambs, or of goats.** (Isaiah 1:11)

GOD AND EPICURUS

Sydney/Carlos: *If God is omnipotent, omniscient and benevolent. Then evil could not continue to exist. If he is omnipotent and omniscient, then he has the knowledge of all evil and the power to end it, but he does not. Then He is not good. If He is omnipotent and benevolent, then He has the power to extinguish evil and wants to do it, for He is good. But he doesn't do it, because he doesn't know how much evil there is, and where evil is. So He is not omniscient. If he is omniscient and good, then he knows all the evil that exists and wants to change it. But this eliminates the possibility of being omnipotent, because if he were, he would eradicate evil. And if He is not omnipotent and omniscient and good, then why call Him God?* (Epicurus)

Reinaldo: Nil, two heads think more than one; with your help we are able to answer all the questions. There are several questions here that I never thought there would be answers. Thanks to your help they are being answered.

Nilvana: Thanks for your consideration, for me it is a surprise that we are able to answer everything, sometimes we are not able to answer because of lack of interest in finding the answers.

Reinaldo/Nilvana: Let's get the answer. God can put an end to evil, but he does not want to. Do you know why? For He would has get rid with us as well, we are evil. If the evil you mention is the devil, He would not fight with a being inferior to Him. (Satan, is Satan of men, not of God) It would be the same as if Superman wanted to fight an ant, it's unfair. That is why in Revelation 20:2 it says that an angel arrested and bound Satan for a thousand years. Likewise, Jesus taught us to overcome Satan in Matthew 4:4 and also in Luke 10:19. He gave us power to tread on serpents, scorpions, and all the strength of the enemy. Evil will not continue to exist; there will come a day when all evil will be destroyed. ***And the devil, which deceived them, was cast into the lake of fire and brimstone, where the beast and the false prophet are; and day and night they will be tormented forever and ever.*** (Revelation 20:14). For now we are have the chance to repent, to change our behavior, and to recognize that we have made a mistake.

(Many Christians are condemning people to hell for futile reasons. Have you done this? Then you are going to hell. Didn't you do it? Then you are going to hell. You're not from my religion? Then you're going to hell. Many say this because they are jealous of sinners who do what they want, while Christians stay only in the will. Stop condemning; don't judge so that you won't be judged. Jesus came to save, and who are we to condemn? Jesus came to save; those who condemns others is making himself greater than Jesus).

IMAGE AND LIKENESS OF GOD

Carlos: ..., "God may put an end to evil, but he does not want it. Do you know why? Because he would have to end us too, because we are evil" -I thought we were the image and likeness of God. Kkk.

Reinaldo/Nilvana: WE WERE, but after man disobeyed, turned away from God, we are no longer his image. God created us his image and likeness, and then with sin we are fallen human beings. There are pure angels and unclean angels, who are called demons (Luke 4:33-35). In our case there are no pure human beings, but only unclean human beings. There is a way for us to purify ourselves by reading and listening to the gospels. ***You are already clean by the word I have spoken to you.*** (John 15:3).

FOOLISH ATHEISTS?

Sidney/Carlos: Psalms 14:1 it says that all those who do not believe in God are fools. Imagine what the world would be like if weren't for those "fools" in physics, biology, literature. Those scientists who won the NOBEL award, do they look foolish to you?

Reinaldo/Nilvana: The verse says: The fool in his heart says. There is no God. Logically these men are intelligent in their areas of performance. I can be an expert in the English language and be a fool in the Japanese language. They are fools for not seeking to know God, but they are wise for seeking to know science.

LISTEN TO VOICES

Sidney/Carlos: It's okay to talk to God. The problem is when God speaks to you. If you hear the "voice" of God, go to see a doctor.

Reinaldo: I partly agree, there are people who say that God talks to them every day and that is an illness. God can talk to anyone, but it is a rare thing. Below I will report my own experience. But first of all the Bible says that God talks to people in some ways, through the Bible, prophets, dreams and in the mind like a voice. In particular, I have had an experience of hearing God's voice.

Nilvana: Is it serious?

Reinaldo: It's serious! Once at Vasp, I was calculating the expenses. When I finished I said to God: Lord, this month I don't know how I will pay my bills. I could felt a voice inside me: in September your tithes will be higher, write in your notebook. I thought it can only be my imagination; the company was firing a lot of people for crises. They fired people with a salary of seven hundred and forty reais (in 2001) to hire others to earn three hundred and seventy. As I was earning four hundred and ninety-nine reais I would have to be satisfied. The voice spoke three times to me saying: In September your tithes will be bigger, write in your notebook. Then I wrote with a very ugly letter, I did not believe. This happened in May 2001, when June fifteen came I went on vacation. A colleague from Vasp, Adriana, called me to work with her in another department where she would be supervisor. She told me: if you come to work with me in Congonhas your salary will be seven hundred and fifty. I accepted, came back from vacation and went to work with her. The August salary was much less than I expected, due to having received vacation discounts. But September came; the salary was already higher as the voice had told me, amounting to seven hundred and fifty reais. That's how what the voice told me was fulfilled. I believe that there are people who are really sick hearing voices. There are people who say they hear voices every day, and God doesn't speak much. In my whole life I think I heard it twice, I believe it was a voice sent from God, not exactly His own voice. God has spoken a lot in the Bible, if we want to hear God speak, let us read the Bible. Especially the new testament, if you don't have time to read the gospel of John, if you don't have time for it, read at least Matthew chapters 5, 6 and 7 that are considered a summary of the bible. When what the voice said to me was fulfilled, I could see that I was not sick.

Nilvana: How interesting! What an experience!

Reinaldo: I remembered an experience that my mother had with God.

Nilvana: You can talk; it's about the voice of God.

Reinaldo: Yes, but she asked God to speak with someone else.

Nilvana: I am curious.

SMS FROM GOD

Reinaldo: Frequently my mother was receiving a visit from a religious person. Every time this person went home, she always gossiped about other people, and this made her upset, my mother didn't want to know about anyone's life. Then one day this person went to my mother´s house to gossip, my mother waited for her to go out, she went into the room and prayed to God: God tells this sister not to come here anymore. The next time they met, this person said to my mother, *"I am not going to your house anymore, that last time I went, after about five minutes, when I was coming to my house, God spoke in my mind like this: Don't go to Margaret's house anymore.*

Nilvana: It's amazing, your mother's faith and experience.

Reinaldo: It impresses me too.

And so we finished the questions.

DESISTANCE

On Monday I entered the "room", waiting for Mr. Sydney's entrance. I waited half an hour and he didn't enter the room. I was at my place of work, at Vasp; I could only wait a total of one hour, because I needed to start working. But on this day he didn't come into the debate room.

The next day I called Nilvana.

-Nil, I'm worried about the x-file issues, it's scientific.

-Don't worry about that.

-You weren't in the debate yesterday, right?

-Yes, I was, but there was no debate, right?

-No, there wasn't, he didn't come in.

-What could have happened?

-I have no idea. They never missed a debate! - Commented Reinaldo.

-But changing the subject, could you help me about a doubt?

-If I can help, I will.

MORE COFFEE

-Could you come here to my house on Sunday?

-Yes, what time?

-Around 4:00 p.m. I would like you to come for afternoon coffee with my family. My mother reinforced the invitation. - She invited Nilvana.

-No problem, I'll be there.

-Bring your Bible; I would like to ask you some questions. It was very pleasant when we were answering together those questions from Mr. Sydney and Carlos. When I answered those questions, others have been raised. I would like you to help me.

-All right Nil, I'll be there. As for being pleasant, I'll say so. It was pleasant for me too, when I was by your side, looking into your eyes, observing your facial expressions, smiling, thinking, dubious, serious and so on.

-Kkk. Rei, I'm shy, I look like a red pepper.

-Even your shyness delights me. You are wonderful.

-Kkk.

-Now I need to sleep. I can't wait to be by your side again. Kiss and bye.

-Kkk. Kiss. Sleep with God's protection. Bye. Kkkkk

-Bye and a kiss.

The most anticipated Sunday came. It was very good that Nil was interested in asking questions. This will make her grow in the knowledge of God too. I arrived there for afternoon coffee with her family. They had a great afternoon coffee. They made cookies, passion fruit cake, couscous, cassava cake, cold cuts, fruits, cream cheese, butter, jelly, tea, coffee, milk, Juliet (kind of homemade cookie) and homemade bread. We were in the kitchen and she called me to the living room, there were three sofas, one with three seats, one with two seats and another with only one seat. We sat on the couch with two seats next to the coffee table; there were some magazines, a notebook and a Bible. Nilvana began to ask some questions.

TELE EVANGELISTS

-Rei, what is your opinion about the tele evangelists.

-Nil, my opinion is not the best, but of course there are always exceptions for everything in life. These preachers are more committed to keeping the TV program than to preaching the gospel; they are obliged to preach what pleases men. They deceive the people into buying the products that pay for the TV program. They are preaching exaggeratedly financial blessing, healing and miracles, they are getting rich unjustly. Jesus said: ***The foxes have dens, and the birds in the air have nests; but the Son of Man has nowhere to lay his head.*** (Matthew 8:20) Jesus had no place to rest. The concern of tele evangelists is to make them buy bibles, but reading is the least important. The preachers that do not have TV programs admire those who are there on TV and end up copying the same kind of adulterated preaching for the goal of keeping the program, full of promises and illusions.

CAMPAIGNS

-I agree with you, for example there are faith campaigns in some churches that are based on the psalms, if it is Psalm 90; you must give an offering of 90 Reais. Why not 90 cents? Why not campaign with Psalm 1?

-Kkk. I laugh, but it's not funny. Imagine if Jesus went to heal someone and started asking, how much money do you have? If you don't have money, get out of line, there is no healing for you. Reinaldo said.

FOR GRACE

-What kind of Jesus is that in some churches? Rei, look here at this verse. Matthew 10:08. ***Heal the sick, raise the dead, cleanse the lepers, cast out demons; you received them for free, for free you will give.***

-My Jesus! My Jesus! My Jesus! ... You have received free, for free you will give. What is happening? Look what Jesus answered in this verse? I don't know what to say, the scene that came to my mind now is of a person taking a punch in the stomach and falling faint on the floor. As if the lie was knocked out by the word of God.

-Was it so impressive?

-It was very impressive. I felt the impact of Jesus' word responding to these churches that say. ... bring your sacrifice ... write your request on the paper and put 50 reais of offering ... and Jesus said, "You received it for free. That is why I realize that there are many atheists because of religion and not because of Jesus.

-This verse: ***Behold, now I know that in all the earth there is no God but in Israel; now I ask you to receive a gift from your servant. But he answered,***

"As the Lord lives, in whose presence I stand, I will not receive it.

Naaman urged him to take it; but he refused. II Kings 5:15-16. Nilvana continued.

-He had cured Naaman and he wanted to give him back a gift and he refused. There are several pastors who are in the media receiving "gifts" for having prayed for someone.

-I understand: if you are really a person who has a special gift from God, like healing for example, even so you should not be charged and not accept payment. Rei, I remembered reading, I don't know where it is writing in the bible about the apostle Paul receiving salary.

APOSTLE PAUL'S SALARY

-Let's see if we can find it in the electronic bible. *Other churches I stripped, receiving wages from them, to serve you; and when I was present with you, and I was in need, I* was *burdensome to no one; for the brethren, when they came from Macedonia, supplied my need; and in all things I kept myself and I will still keep myself from being heavy to you.* (2Cor 11:8 and 9). Reinaldo informed.

-The apostle Paul, as a missionary, having to travel to several countries needed salary, money for his missions and to keep himself, of course. On the other hand, he explains that he didn't want to be financial heavy to anyone, he didn't exploit, and he didn't get rich for it.

-To complement this note: *we didn't even eat anyone's bread for free, but with labor and fatigue we worked night and day so as not to be heavy at any of you.* (II Thessalonians 3:8)

-Now I felt the impact. *It is fulfilled: I am the Alpha and the Omega, the beginning and the end. Everyone who is thirsty, I will give him <u>free</u> to drink from the fountain of the water of life*. (Revelation 21:6). -completed Nilvana

-Why for free? Because for God money has no value, it is free because nobody can pay! God does not need money, the work of God needs, which would be to help the people, the neediest.

Her family was still in the kitchen finishing the coffee, so I spoke to Nilvana very quietly so that only she would listen.

-How good it is to be here with you, how wonderful.

She moved her head saying yes, looked at the kitchen and came back to me and also said very quietly.

-It's good for me too.

She cleared her throat. Then she made a comment to me.

DARK MAGIC AND INNOCENCE

-Rei, I watched a report talking about a man who put more than 30 needles in a child's body. When they showed the criminal, I was surprised. He seemed to be a very humble, kind and simple person. When I saw him I could feel that he wouldn't hurt a fly. Was he pretending? If he was really pretending he is an excellent actor.

-I also saw this report. I believe that man is really a very good person, but he did a terrible thing because of religion. They asked him to do it for dark magic ritual. His neighborhood wanted to kill him because they did not understand that he was influenced by a false religion. There are people who commit crimes because they are really bad. Others because they have their heads easily influenced. The most interesting thing I saw was in the end, he said with tears: *I know that not even God will forgive me for what I did.* Nil, he showed repentance and without him knowing God already forgave him, because it was true, it came from the heart.

-Then the media announced him like a monster. I believe he has received forgiveness from God. For God is incomparably greater than our sins and forgives the sincerely repentant. Help me with a doubt, many Christians say that God is greater than any sin and can forgive. But most say that if someone commits suicide, he has no chance of salvation, he will go straight to hell. What do you have to say about that? Nilvana asked.

SUICIDE

-First of all, there will be no one in "hell" until Jesus rules the earth in the millennium. As for suicide, I have heard opinions about the following: Imagine if you were in a forest and a lion was about to kill you. In front of you there is a huge waterfall fall, and you know that if you jump, you will die or commit suicide. So in this case you had no guilt, no option, it was not a condemnatory suicide. Now, if you were a thief running from the police, an unrepentant sinner, then it would be a condemnatory suicide. I wouldn't advise anyone to suicide for any reason. God always gives us a "light at the end of the tunnel".

LET THEM TAKE

-How would you react to a robbery?

-According to Jesus and the security experts have spoken the following: *give them whatever they ask and even more. **...and to whoever wants to plead with you, and take off your tunic, let them take off his cloak too;*** (Matthew 5:40). Overcome evil with good and not with evil. -Replied Reinaldo.

FEAR OF DEATH

-Are you afraid to die?

-No, they say that cat has seven lives.

-You are funny guy, aren´t you?

-Sometimes yes, sometimes no, we shouldn't be afraid, if we have a good heart at peace with God and believe in the saving grace of Jesus, there is nothing to fear. Whoever believes in Him will just sleep a little longer and then rise to eternal life. -Reinaldo answered.

-But changing the subject, I was reading a book by a famous psychologist and writer here in Brazil. He said that the human brain is more complex than the universe itself, isn't that a bit too much?

OUR BRAIN AND THE UNIVERSE

-Yes, it's wonderful, some scientists say that. When we look at the universe and see billions of galaxies with billions of stars in which there is no life, we wonder: Why did God create all this? All without life, what's the reason of all this? Let's compare, our brain has about 100 billion neurons and if I was nanoscopic and lived in one of these neurons, I would also say that all the other neurons would be a great waste of space. We know in fact all neurons are part of something bigger, our brain. So imagine Nil, if the whole universe is just the brain of God. There are scholars who say that the universe looks a lot like the brain.

-Wow Rei, you took my breath away. Our mind cannot imagine the size of the universe. We can have a little notion; listen to this comparison that I will read to you: The speed of light surrounds our planet seven times in only one second and at that same absurd speed it would take about 14 billion years to go from the beginning to the end of the universe.

-Wow Nil, you took my breath away too.

-They knowing the complexity of life, why they don't believe in God.

CHRISTIAN SCIENTISTS

-Not all scientists are atheists! Almost 40% are scientists who believe in God. Mr. Francis Collins (director of the human genome) said about the percentage of scientists who believe in God. *What about spiritual belief among scientists? Actually, it is more common than many people imagine. In 1916, researchers asked biologists, physicists and mathematicians if they believed in a God who communicates actively with humanity and to whom it is possible to pray, in the hope of receiving an answer. About 40% of them answered yes. In 1997, the same study was repeated literally, it surprised the researchers; the percentage remained very close to the previous one.* (**The language of God**, pg. 12) As for the complexity you mentioned. I remembered something I saw in a documentary. Scientists were working on the assembly of a robot and said that to program a robot to make a simple gesture, such as a wave goodbye, it requires a great complexity in both programming and mechanics. I believe that trying to assemble a robot we realize how complex the human being is.

-I didn't know that there were scientists who believe in God. It's good to know that. Nilvana commented.

DIFFICULTY IN BELIEVING (2)

-Sometimes believe in God is not as easy as it seems. Even Jesus' disciples gave proof that they did not believe in Him as they should. *Later Jesus appeared to the Eleven as they were eating; he rebuked them for their lack of faith and their stubborn refusal to believe those who had seen him after he had risen.* (Mark 16:14). Reinaldo commented.

-I remembered another verse that says so: *No one can come to me unless the Father who sent me draws them, and I will raise them up at the last day.* (John 6: 44)

ONE BAIT FOR EACH FISH

-The Word of God fills my spirit. It is with the Word of God that we can help them. It has the right "bait" for every "fish".

-If each fish is caught with a different bait. What would be the strategy to talk about God in Africa? I say the poorest parts of this continent.

-I would talk about the hope that Jesus gave us about heaven. There will be no hunger, death or pain there.. ***There will be no more death' or mourning or crying or pain, for the old order of things has passed away… The wall was made of jasper, and the city of pure gold, as pure as glass*** (Revelation 21:4 and 18). And I would give food too; I would say that we are temporarily poor. Imagine if someone comes to you and asks you for something to eat and you answer: Go in peace, I will pray for you. kkk.

-Kkk. It is a joke, isn´t it? Kkk.

-For me it sounds like a joke. Kkk.

-The apostle James said about this: ***Suppose a brother or a sister is without clothes and daily food. If one of you says to them, "Go in peace; keep warm and well fed," but does nothing about their physical needs, what good is it?*** (James 2:15,16). -Nilvana commented.

-What would be a strategy to talk about Jesus in India?

-In India several gods are worshiped. I could preach about the chapter seven until the eleven of Exodus. God sent plagues to Egypt; each plague was related to a god, so God showed that their gods had no power. The wizards recognized that it was the action of the God's finger (Exodus 8:19). God with one finger destroyed all Egyptian gods.

GOD DEFEATED THE GODS

-How plagues are gods-related?

-1º the god Hapi, the protector of the River Nile, was humiliated when God made the waters turn to blood and after stink. Where was the "protector of the Nile," where was the power of God Hapi?

2º the goddess Hekt, symbolized by a frog, was humiliated when a plague of frogs appeared from the Nile, and this goddess could not control them and keep them in the river.

-Could you name the others?

-Yes, 3º the dust was considered sacred and when performing the rituals, their clothes should be clean, without the presence of insects. When the dust turned into lice it was not possible to perform the rituals. In this third plague there is no specific god, but as all gods demanded rituals, they were all no longer worshipped. Nobody can perform rituals with insects.

The 4th god Beelzebub, who was scaring the flies away, was humiliated when God sent the plague of flies and these flies made their life miserable.

5th the god Amon, protector of the flocks, was humiliated when God sent a plague to destroy the animals.

6th the god Tiphon, protector of the wounds, was humiliated when God sent the plague of ulcers; the priests themselves were the first to acquire ulcers.

7th the goddess, Serafis, protector of the crops, was humiliated when God sent the plague of hail, which destroyed the plants and crops. Those who believe in the world of God sheltered the harvest and the animals and they were saved from the hail.

8º the goddesses, Serafis and Isis, protectors of the vegetation, were humiliated when the locusts ate what was left of the plantation caused by the hail.

9º the god Ra, symbolized by the sun, was humiliated when God brought dense darkness to Egypt, especially Pharaoh himself acclaimed being god´s son, was humiliated.

10º (no relation with gods) the Egyptians killed Hebrew children at the time of Moses' birth, now God also decides to kill (in fact he took their lives, there was no pain, they were sleeping) the firstborn son, whose houses did not have the mark of the blood of the lamb on their doors.

So, with the ten plagues, He showed that He was above the gods of Egypt. He showed that His power is above any gods. God interfered in the area where each god "dominated".

(All the plagues could have been avoided if Pharaoh had freed the descendants of Abraham, a people who had the promise of the Promised Land. Was God's evil? For love of the Egyptians he warned first, giving the option for all the plagues to be avoided. Some people say that from the first plague to the last one it took a year, that is, they had time to repent. There was no violence in the death of the firstborns sons, they were sleeping, and it was already midnight. He who gave his life is the only one who has the right to take it, and he did it in the best way possible, while they were sleeping).

-God of gods! How wonderful! It is very good to know that the time of repentance that God gave was a demonstration of love for them.

-When this conscience, the love of God, takes hold of our being we will know God for real.

-How would you preach about Jesus in Holland? In Holland prostitutes are exposed in glass windows with their price.

-I don't know what I would say, but to call the people attention, I would put an old lady in a glass display case, without beauty with the value of 999.999.999.999.999.999.999.999.999.999.999.9 99. ...of euros, with three points at the end, i.e. an infinite value. I would put the site for people to find out why that old lady with no looks is worth so much. I would put an answer like this on the site: our value to God is so great that he sent his only son, Jesus, to pay our due value.

-God valued us too much when he sent his only son, Jesus.

WHEN WILL BE THE END?

-What about the end of the world, do you believe it is related to earthquakes?

-Some say that the number of earthquakes has not increased, but the number of seismographs. But there are places where people are feeling the earthquake without needing seismographs. Where there were no quakes now there are. Like here in Brazil, there were no earthquakes, but tremors were felt here from distant earthquakes. I heard another day a theologian saying that there have been more earthquakes in the last 10 years than in the last 100 years, an impressive fact. Jesus said it is not a sign of the end, but the beginning of pain. - said Reinaldo.

-What else do you have to say about the end of the world?

-Look at this matter. So far, since the year "1,000 A.D., we have had 28 predictions that the world would end, including the prediction for 2012 and another prediction for 2033. In the prediction are involved theologians, astrologers, apocalyptic theorists, Egyptologists. The curious thing is that in 1939, the Second World War broke out, the closest thing to the apocalypse, but nobody made any prediction. We can see that they all failed. Some predictions are involving some kind of cataclysmic event". Some attribute these errors to the Bible. But the Bible says it does not depend on an event, but depends on a message for the end to come. ***And this gospel of the kingdom will be preached all over the world in witness to all nations, and then the end will come.*** (Matthew 24: 14)

-It is difficult to hear the words of Jesus, the gospel, what we are hearing most is about the Old Testament, about prosperity, offering and tithes. - Nilvana added.

-So Nil, if you are talking about the Old Testament instead of the gospel of Jesus, the end will never come. I believe the gospel will be preached all over the world after the rapture, because they will know that Jesus has raptured thousands of people and they will only talk about the gospel, about Jesus' love. There will be no space to talk about anything but repentance, salvation, the love of God and the gospel itself.

-Unfortunately it is true. In Matthew 23:23 there is a part of the verse that says the following: ***Woe to you,*** *scribes and Pharisees, hypocrites! For you decimate mint, dill, and cumin, and despise the most important of the law, justice, mercy, and faith.*

-Yes, mercy is linked to forgiveness, goodness, love of neighbor. Faith is linked to hope. It is interesting that in 1 Corinthians 13:13 the apostle Paul confirms this. *Now then, faith, hope and love remain, these three, but the greatest of these is love.* - completed Reinaldo.

-I liked the statements, quoted by the Lord Jesus himself and the apostle Paul.

-But we were talking about the prediction of Jesus' return. Have you ever heard of a prediction from the president of the world biblical society?

-No, but it seems interesting to me because it is about the president of the world biblical society. I've been told that this man has five doctorates in theology, that is, a lot of credibility in biblical matters. - Nilvana said.

-Yes, Doctor F. Kenton Beshore, is based on the rebirth of the State of Israel in 1948. *Then he proposed a parable to them: Look at the fig tree, and at all the trees; when they begin to sprout, you know for yourselves, when you see them, summer is already approaching. So you too, when you see these things happening, know that the kingdom of God is near. Truly, I say to you, this generation will*

not pass away until all these things are accomplished. (Luke 21:29-32). -Commented Reinaldo.

-Now that you mentioned I am remembered it. The people of Israel are represented by the fig tree in the bible, according to Psalms 90:10 a generation is from seventy to eighty years old. ***Our lifetimes are seventy years; and if some, for their robustness, reach eighty years...*** Then the fig tree (Israel) began to sprout in 1948, a time when Israel was considered a nation by the UN, a generation can vary from seventy to eighty years, that is, 1948 + 70 = 2018 or 1948 + 80 = 2028. The return of Christ will occur until 2028 and the rapture until 2021 because the rapture will occur seven years before the coming of Christ.

-You understand perfectly. Currently the life expectancy in Israel is close to 83 years, if we were to consider this current data and not that of the Bible it would be 2024 maximum. -Reinaldo answered.

-On the other hand, Jesus also said in Matthew 24:36 that no one knows the day or the hour.

-The day and the hour nobody knows, however, the approximate time is possible to know. For example, if I told you that next year I would buy a car. I'm can say that because until then I will have enough money, but the day and the hour I don't know, I need to research, prices, brands, etc. The day I don't know, but the year I know. In my opinion, this is what Jesus said: **"But the day and the hour, no one knows, neither the angels in heaven nor the Son, but the Father.** (Mark 13:32)

-It is different between knowing the year and knowing the day and hour. - said Nilvana.

-Exactly. There are several verses to base on this theory, but I'll quote only two.

-Ok. That's enough. Where are they?

-In Psalms 90:4 it says: **A <u>thousand</u> years in your sight are like a day that has just gone by, or like a <u>watch</u> in the night**- quoted Reinaldo.

The night is divided into four watches for the Jews.

1st watch (1000 years) 1st millennium 6:00 pm to 9:00 pm

2nd watch (2000 years) 2nd millennium 21:00 pm to **00:00**

3rd watch (3000 years) 3rd millennium **00:00** to 03:00 am

Jesus said that the fiance would come at **midnight,** Matthew 25:6. **At midnight the cry rang out: 'Here's the bridegroom! Come out to meet him!** At midnight is the transition between the second and third millennium, the time we are living in now. If we consider two thousand years after Christ's death, it will be 2033, but our calendar is almost five years late, that is, 2033 - 5 = 2028 - 7 (the rapture occurs 7 years before the coming of Jesus) = 2021, again the same date appears as the logic of the birth of Israel.

-For me this is the most convincing theory.

-Among other things, Dr. F. Kenton Beshore (president of the world biblical society, has 5 doctorates in theology, studies the bible for over 65 years) highlights: five "fundamental" prophetic events are already occurring today: the "fall" or apostasy of the church, (certainly) increase of knowledge, (no doubt) growth of anti-Semitism, development of technology for the mark of the beast (there is a technological prediction for 2019 that will be implanted a chip in our brain so that we can access the Internet, this may be the mark of the beast, because it is not only a chip, but a chip implanted in the brain that will be able to influence our will.) Finally, Israel is attacked by an alliance of Islamic nations with Russia. I believe 50% in this theory.

-Why not 100%? - asked Nilvana.

-Because man can make mistakes in his interpretations.

MEGA TEMPLE

-I believe that Jesus is really coming back because the gospel is being preached all over the world. Here in Brazil it is really growing, there are a lot of churches.

Near my house I noticed that they opened about ten churches in less than a year. Not to mention the mega temples, so the gospel is really being preached. -Nilvana commented.

-I'm sorry to disappoint you, but I don't believe most churches are preaching the gospel that Jesus commanded them to preach. Mega temples are built with the money of the people, in order to raise more money and impress the people even more. Jesus said that many false prophets would arise and deceive many (Matthew 7:15). The number of churches is growing, and on the other hand, robberies are growing, because the church no longer preaches that you should not steal. The number of divorced couples and betrayals has grown, because the church no longer preaches on the subject of family. The violence has grown because the church does not preach any more than you should hit one side of the face you should offer the other and so on. The issue that reigns is material prosperity, these issues that do not encourage the collection of money are "forgotten" in most churches. - commented Reinaldo.

At this moment Nilvana's mother called her.

LET'S WASH THE DISHES

-Nil, can you take a break and help me wash the dishes? –Asked Nilvana´s mother.

-Yes, Mom. Rei, if you want to watch TV while I help my mother make yourself at home.

-Mrs. Nilza, let me help her, I'll help Nilvana with the dishes.

-No son, you're a visitor, you don't have to do that.

-No, you can let me, I've been helping my mother with household chores, not much, sometimes, let me at least sweep the kitchen and dry the dishes.

-Only this time, I'm late to go to church, so I'll agree with you. -Mrs. Nilza answered.

We got up and went to the kitchen.

-How many dishes to wash Nil, we'll be late for service. - said Reinaldo.

-No, I'll wash everything quickly and I´ll clean everything too.

-Let's begin, let´s do this. Where's the broom?

-It's behind this door there. - Nilvana answered.

We started tidying up the kitchen and continued with our conversation. Nilvana asked.

IDENTIFYING A FALSE PROPHET

-What would be the main characteristics of false prophets for you?

-Jesus said that by their fruits you will know them, that is, what they are producing, what are their works, how they are acting? Are they acting with love, mercy, forgiveness? Nil, read Matthew 23, you will see what false prophets are like. In summary this chapter shows that they are linked more to rituals and the law than to justice, mercy and faith (faith in God, not faith in faith or objects).

-If that is the case, we are surrounded by false prophets and every day one more appears.

-Yes, there are few churches that are still preaching the gospel of Jesus. - Reinaldo answered.

-Rei, do you want more coffee? I just warmed up some more.

-Yes, a little more, please.

-Here it is.

-Thank you.

-You're welcome. Rei, so there are few places to worship God, since most churches are not preaching the gospel.

-Perhaps I'll let you down one more time.

-Why?

THE PLACE OF WORSHIP

-There is no place defined by Jesus to worship God. When Jesus was talking to a Samaritan woman, she asked this question. The woman asked, ***"Our fathers worshiped on this mountain, and you say that in Jerusalem is the place to worship.*** (John 4:20) Jesus answered: ... ***neither on this mountain nor in Jerusalem will you worship the Father? The true worshipers will worship the Father in spirit and in truth;*** (John 4:21 and 23) - said Reinaldo.

-In spirit and in truth, what does it mean?

-In spirit it means, without limit, without barriers, without an appointment, without a determined place, it is at any time and in any place. And in truth, it means IN TRUTH.

-Truth is truth. Kkk. So there is no place? What about the churches? On the other hand, at home it is difficult to find a time; there are many distractions like the internet, TV, cell phone, children and so on. It is not the same thing. - commented Nilvana.

-That depends, in the church there are also many distractions. Reserve a moment when only you are at home, a moment when you know that nobody will interrupt you.

-Maybe the only time I could be free of this would be at dawn.

WHAT CLEANSES OUR SOUL?

-Oops! I almost broke a plate. If it really is a church that preaches the gospel, then we will be cleansed. ***You are already cleansed by the word I have spoken to you.*** (John 15:3). Worshiping God extends to daily life, that is, you are watching TV, sweeping a house, washing a dish, make it a praise to God. How you deal with your neighbor is the best way, not the only way to worship God. - said Reinaldo.

-The gospel cleanses us, you said this to Zilda.

-Speaking in a place Jesus said, ***"But you, when you pray enter your room and, closing the door, pray to your Father who is in secret; and your Father, who sees in secret, will publically reward you.*** (Matthew 6:6)

-Tell me something, do you believe that God can grant us anything?

-Yes, but God is not wizard.

-What do you mean? - asked Nilvana.

BLESSINGS

-There are people who think that God can do a magic to solve their problems. God makes miracles and not magic. There are cases where He makes miracles. But most of the time He does not. For example: When God promised the promise land to the people of Israel, they had to fight for it. When God sent the prophet Samuel to anoint David to King, a red carpet did not immediately appear for him to take the throne. He was prepared and trained to be King.

-It is true Rei. God helps us and enables us, so that, the blessings or miracles are fulfilled in our lives.

-Dependent on the kind of miracle you want to achieve it can take years. In the meantime He will prove your heart; He will see whether you love more, the blessings or the Blesser. He wants us to recognize him as the most important Being in our lives. Why do we think the blessings are taking so long? Why are we so anxious? If we have his presence as the greatest of blessings, we would not be so anxious. If we love him with all our heart, time will pass faster. It does not mean that the "clock" will accelerate. Time is relative; if we put our finger on the fire for one minute it will seem like an eternity. If I am talking to you Nil, as I do now, ten minutes will seem like ten seconds. Love has the power to shorten time. - said Reinaldo.

LOTTERY WINNERS AND THE RICH

-How romantic you are! Speaking of material goods, I remembered a survey they did about the biggest lottery winners in the United States. After ten years they went to ask how the experience of getting rich. Most of them said it would have been better if they hadn't won the prize. It was good at that moment, but they didn't know how to manage. Many of them were poorer than before they won the prize. –said Reinaldo

-Do you believe that the rich have to give everything to the poor to be saved?

-No, a rich guy asked Jesus what he should do to be saved. Jesus said, ***"He must keep the commandments, not kill, not steal, not commit adultery, love his neighbor, love God above all"***. It was enough for him to keep the commandments, but he asked "*what more I need to do*?" it seems he wanted to show him up. So, Jesus answered, ***"If you want to be <u>perfect</u> sell everything give it to the poor, follow me and you will have treasure in heaven"*** (Matthew 19:16-22).

-Ah! So the act of giving everything to the poor is not to be saved, it would be if he wanted to be perfect.

-Exactly, we are saved by God's grace revealed in Jesus. The rich don't need to give everything, give something to the poor, help some charities, show love to others by helping financially. Not only the rich, the less poor should help the poor.

-The most important question for the rich would be: How are you getting rich? Honestly or harming others? Are you spending your money on things that displease God?

HOW MUCH IS JESUS WORTH?

-I believe that God can give us anything as long as it is less valuable than Jesus.

-I don't understand, by any chance there is something more valuable than Jesus Christ that God can't give us? - asked Nilvana.

-No, there is nothing greater than Jesus Christ. For example, 1,000 "zillions" of Euros is infinitely smaller than Jesus, nothing can compare to Him, and this number is only to help our imagination. What I mean is, God has already given us Jesus, He is the greater value, so He can give us anything.

-Now I understand. He can give us absolutely everything.

NEITHER WEALTH NOR POVERTY

-No, I mean that God can give everything as long as the person does not value that thing above Jesus. *For life is more than food, and the body more than clothes.* (Luke 12:23). He gave the life that is more important than the sustenance, how can He not give the sustenance? He gave the body that is more important than the garments, how will he not give the garment? God gave His only son who is more important than everything, how can He not give us everything we need? I am not talking about riches. We don't need much to live well. *Give me neither poverty nor wealth; only give me the necessary food. If not, having too much, I would deny you and leave you, and say: Who is the Lord? If I became poor, I could steal, thus dishonoring the name of my God* (Prov. 30:8-9). After Jesus died for our sins, we sinners, have free access to God. We do not need to ask anyone to pray for us, if you want to pray for someone ok, there is no problem. But we all have access to God through Jesus Christ. Imagine that in front of you there is an abyss that is called sin and there on the other side is God, we cannot get there, but God gave us a bridge that is called Jesus Christ to have access to Him.

(I recommend that you do not attend churches that talk a lot about blessings and promises, this causes a lot of anxiety and psychological illness. It is the kind of church that can make a lot of money. Attend a church that uses more the New Testament, which teaches you to love God and your neighbor, which talks about salvation through repentance, forgiveness, where there is social service to the neediest, this is the purpose of being a church).

-Very well, you were deep. Can I ask a question about the debate with Zilda. - Nilvana said.

-If I can help you, I will.

TWO JESUS

-I was curious about something in the debate with Zilda. You said she believes in the historical Jesus. Are they not the same?

-Yes, they are the same Jesus, with two profiles, one from the tradition and the other from archaeology.

1) Tradition> Birth: He was born in year 1, in Bethlehem.

Archaeology> Birth: He was born between 6 and 4 B.C. in Nazareth.

-Jesus: Born in Bethlehem and not in Nazareth according to the Bible (Matthew 2:1). I also agree with the year of birth according to archaeology. For the monk Dionysius Exigus, made a mistake in the Christian calendar by replacing it with the Roman calendar. In other words, our calendar is on average 5 years late.

-That is another thing I didn't know about.

2) Tradition>Schooling: High level of education, with the ability to read and interpret erudite text.

Archaeology>Schooling: Illiterate like most peasants. That did not prevent knowing the traditions orally.

-We know that at least Jesus knew how to read. In Luke 4:16-19 he says, ***"And when he came to Nazareth, where he had been brought up, he went into the synagogue on a Sabbath day, as he was accustomed to, and stood up to read.***

-At that time it was something admirable to know how to read.

3) Tradition> Religion: Jewish.

Archaeology> Religion: Jewish.

4) Tradition> Family circle: Only son of Mary conceived by the Holy Spirit.

Archaeology> Family circle: Son of Joseph and Mary surrounded by several brothers.

-I agree with both. In Luke 1:34-35 Mary responds to the angel who could not have a son because he had no relationship with any man. Then the angel said that he would be called son of the Most High. And also the angel answers Joseph that the son will be begotten by Holy Spirit (Matthew 1:20). And in Matthew 12:46, Mark 3:31 and John 8:19 talk about his mother and his brothers. Now, naturally there is sexual intercourse in marriage, Joseph and Mary only waited for Jesus to be born so that they could have a normal sexual life, like any other couple (Matthew 1:25). There is nothing wrong about this.

In this verse he said that Jose did not know (sexually speaking) Mary until she gave birth to her firstborn, Jesus.

5) Tradition> Civil Status: Celibacy.

Archaeology> Civil status: There is no evidence that Jesus was married. But every religious leader had a woman.

-In this profile there is no biblical or archaeological evidence that He was married. There is only one supposition on the part of archaeology. There is the apocryphal gospel of Philip saying that Jesus was married. This gospel was written in the third century (less than 300 years after Jesus' birth) the gospels in the Bible were written in the first century (less than 100 years after Jesus' birth). Nil, now I will ask you, which of the two is more reliable?

-How much closer are the writings to the events the most reliable is. It is the same as reading something your "children", that is, your contemporaries wrote about you. And to read something that your great-great-great-great-grandchild wrote about you. - replied Nilvana.

-Exactly, that's it. Nil, if one day they proved that Jesus was married and had children, it would not shake up my faith. What is the problem?

-It's not a problem for me either. Although I believe that he didn't get married because the gospels don't report it.

6) Tradition> Physical traits: The West has fixed its image as that of a European.

Archaeology> Physical traits: According to researchers it would have the appearance of an Arab.

-In this profile I agree with archaeology, He was not blond with blue eyes.

-I also agree, this image of blond Jesus with blue eyes is from Hollywood movies. Nilvana said.

7) Tradition> Death: The Roman Empire shook.

Archaeology>Death: If there were a newspaper it would be unlikely that his death would be published.

-What would be shaking? I believe that the Roman Empire was shaken in the sense that they were not able to end Christianity. And later Christianity became the official religion of the Roman Empire.

-As for publishing, I believe it would be more likely than unlikely to be published. For the simple fact that a man drew crowds with signs and miracles he did. This publication would also depend on the type of interest of who would publish. Would the media of that time be impartial? Or would it only publish the interests of the Roman Empire? For me it is the second option.

-Surely it is the second option, until today the media are influenced by the powerful.

EVIL SPIRITS

-Have you ever seen a spiritual being, an angel or demons? - asked Nilvana.

-I "saw" three demons. Once, my neighbor rented the house to people whose religion was Quimbanda. They spent from Saturday afternoon to Sunday morning drumming. Once, Sunday morning when I was waking up, I hadn´t opened my eyes yet, I was aware that I was awake. It was at this moment that I "saw" an evil spirit sitting on my bed, crossed, near …

To be continue on the 3/3

REFERENCES

http://webcache.googleusercontent.com/search?q=cache:qBhuHcyppk8J:top10mais.org/top-10-evidencia-existencia-jesus-cristo/+&cd=1&hl=pt-BR&ct=clnk&gl=br

Revista - Galileu, "A guerra do sudário", Pablo Nogueira, abril de 2003, pág. 25.

http://webcache.googleusercontent.com/search?q=cache:e9-odZ5Li-wJ:www.nunes3373eb.com/news/a100-quatrilh%25C3%25B5es-de-chances-porque-yeshua-e-o-messias/+&cd=1&hl=pt-BR&ct=clnk&gl=br

https://rationalwiki.org/wiki/Extraordinaryclaimsrequireextraordinaryevidence

http://diascomuns.blogspot.com.br/2011/05/george-collin.html

https://citacoes.in/autores/frederick-douglas/

(https://caiafarsa.wordpress.com/igreja-mais-antiga-do-mundo-deixa-teologos-espantados-2/igreja-mais-antiga-do-mundo-deixa-teologos-espantados/)

(https://noticias.gospelprime.com.br/arqueologia-ruinas-sinagoga-jesus/).

https://www.bibliaonline.com.br

http://saude.ig.com.br/alimentacao-bemestar/2013-11-22/14-alimentos-que-combatem-o-cansaco.html

(**) Revista - National Geographic, "Os assombrosos mundos do interior da célula", Rick Gore, setembro de 1976, pp. 357, 358, 360.

Revista - Veja, "O fim do mundo", André Petry de Nova York, novembro de 2009, pág. 94 e 95.

Revistas - Super interessante, "30 maiores mistérios da ciência", Rodrigo Cavalcante, junho de 2007, pág. 25.

Livro - Instituto teológico Quadrangular-Introdução a bíblia Rev. Marco A. T. Lapa.

https://webcache.googleusercontent.com/search?q=cache:Jbr9atwDqy4J:https://www.caiofabio.net/conteudo_detalhe.php?codigo=04563+&cd=3&hl=pt-BR&ct=clnk&gl=br

(**) Livro - Heredity and the Nature of man, pág. 126

http://tdibrasil.org/index.php/2016/01/25/problema -5-aparecimento-abrupto-especies-registro-fossil- nao-condiz-evolucao/

(**) Livro - Os peixes, F.D. Ommanney, pág. 65.

(**) Field museum of natural history bulletin, Chicago, EUA, "Conflitos entre Darwin e a Paleontologia", de David M. Raup, Janeiro de 1979, pág. 23

Revista - Escola, A origem da vida, Anderson Moço, com colaboração de Bianca Bibiano e Rodrigo Ratier, abril de 2009, pág. 36/37. (fontes: José Manuel Martins, professor de biologia, a ciência da biologia de William K. Purves e outros.

Jornal da tarde, Jamil Chade, 31 de março de 2010. pág. 13 A.

Jornal diario de S. Paulo, Aline Mustafa, 21 de maio de 2010, pág. 10.

Livro - "A vida - Qual a sua origem?", copyright 1985 by watch tower bible and tract society of Pennsylvania (U.S.A.) pág. 131, 132, 204-207

(**) Livro - Missing links (Elos que faltam) de John Reader, 1981, pp 109,110; Hen´s Teeth and horse´s toes (Dentes de Galinha e casco de Cavalo), de Stephen Jay Gould, 1983, pp. 201-226.

(**) Livro - A origem da vida, de John D. Bernal, 1967, pág. 144

(**) Livro - Evolution From Space, pág. 24.

http://www.criacionismo.com.br/2008/10/archaeopt eryx-ave-extinta-ou-forma.html

(**) Livro - New scientist, Darwismo no próprio começo da vida, de Leslie Orgel, 15 de abril, 1982, pág. 151.

Revista - Veja, "Os segredos da memória", Diogo Schelp, janeiro de 2010, pág. 82.

Livro - "A vida - Qual a sua origem?", copyright 1985 by watch tower bible and tract society of Pennsylvania (U.S.A.)

http://www.cienciamao.usp.br/tudo/exibir.php?midi a=t2k&cod=_ciencias_05cie

Revista - Galileu, "Eles querem Deus na ciência", Marília Coutinho, agosto de 2001, pág. 33. (coluna)

Enciclopédia Barsa eletrônica. (Editorial Planeta)

Revista - Galileu, "O Deus de Einstein", Marcelo Damato, Novembro de 2007, pág. 50.

Revista - Escola, A origem da vida, Anderson Moço, com colaboração de Bianca Bibiano e Rodrigo Ratier, abril de 2009, pág. 33.

Livro - O mestre do amor / Você é insubstituível – Augusto Cury (https://m.youtube.com/watch?v:=ubp6010z=ozoD0)

Bíblia - Traduzida por João Ferreira de Almeida

https://www.bibliaonline.com.br/acf/lc/1

https://www.biblegateway.com

Tradutores/translators

https://www.deepl.com/pt-BR/translator

https://www.reverso.net/translationresults.aspx?lang=PT&direction=portugues-ingles

L.C.C. - Publicações Eletrônicas http://www.culturabrasil.pro.br/ Versão para e Book eBooksBrasil.com

Pregação em DVD- Myles Munroe – Governando seu domínio pessoal

http://webcache.googleusercontent.com/search?q=cache:TVVKjrrHdbcJ:www.dc.golgota.org/estudos/plagio.html+&cd=1&hl=pt-BR&ct=clnk&gl=br

https://webcache.googleusercontent.com/search?q=cache:URT_WCxlnROJ:https://dicmouer.com/2013/01/27/as-coincidencias-entre-lincoln-e-kennedy/+&cd=6&hl=pt-BR&ct=clnk&gl=br

https://ateu.wordpress.com/2007/12/01/60-perguntas-que-farao-de-voce-um-ateu/

http://gracamaior.com.br/mensagens/128-as-10-pragas-do-egito-e-sua-relacao-com-as-divindades-pagas-egipcias

http://gracamaior.com.br/mensagens/128-as-10-pragas-do-egito-e-sua-relacao-com-as-divindades-pagas-egipcias.html&usg=ALkJrhhF34nWTcm0NsYRPsQTYAC8A1qEBA
Mensagens

http://www.youtube.com/watch?v=kHkjmifqWkA

https://www.youtube.com/results?search_query=zeitgeist+refutado+caio+fabio

https://www.youtube.com/watch?v=a-2HBSfPZpU

https://noticias.gospelprime.com.br/kenton-beshore-sbm-arrebatamento-volta-de-jesus-2018-2028/

http://www.oarrebatamento.net/a-palavra-nas-escrituras/evidencias-biblicas-revelam-a-epoca-da-volta-de-jesus.html

www.vemevetv.com.br (Um canal no Youtube que mais me ajudou, com o reverendo Caio Fabio)

** As referências com 2 asteriscos foram extraídas das referências do livro "A vida - Qual a sua origem? ", copyright 1985 by watch tower bible and tract society of Pennsylvania (U.S.A.)